BOOK TWO IN THE SPRINGVILLE TRILOGY

THE SON OF A GHOST

A SPICY ROMANCE NOVEL

BY: AMBER RODRIGUEZ

Copyright © 2025 by Amber Rodriguez

All rights reserved.

No part of this publication may be reproduced, distributed, or transmitted in any form or by any means, including photocopying, recording, or other electronic or mechanical methods, without the prior written permission of the publisher, except as permitted by U.S. copyright law. For permission requests, contact Amber Rodriguez at ambermrodriguez@gmail.com

No portion of this book may be used to feed or train AI generators or data bases

The story, all names, characters, and incidents portrayed in this production are fictitious. No identification with actual persons (living or deceased), places, buildings, and products is intended or should be inferred.

Book Cover by Amber Rodriguez

Paperback ISBN: 9798989923243

Ebook ISBN: 9798989923250

Website:www.amrbooks.com

First edition 2026

Contents

Dedication	1
Other works by Amber Rodriguez	3
Author's Note	5
Trigger Warnings	7
The Son of a Ghost Playlist	9
1. PROLOUGE	13
2. Welcome to Springville	19
3. She's off limits	39
4. The Church, The Brunch, & The Lawyer's Office	57
5. God's Cruel Jokes and Mangos	73

6. Faith, Pain, & A Little Bit of Pleasure	91
7. Keeping Promises Has Never Been So Hard	109
8. Who Wakes up Looking This Good?	125
9. An Addiction & My Best friend's Baby Shower	139
10. A Sex Demon, A Grand Re-opening, & My Ex is Here?	155
11. My Family is Embarrassing Me & He Loves it	171
12. A Big Family Doesn't Seem So Bad	187
13. With Her	203
14. She Liked Her Surprise & Now We're Going Thrifting	219
15. Revelations & Goodbyes	237
16. A Stubborn Woman, Death, & Danny	255
17. Death Comes in Three's	269
18. Epilogue	287
19. Extended Epilogue	293

Author's Note	299
About the Author	303
The Son of a Ghost Discussion Guide	305

Dedication

Sweet, Religious filth. That's it. That's the dedication.

Other works by Amber Rodriguez

<u>StandAlone</u>

Beautiful Chaos

<u>Springville Trilogy</u>

The Son of a Pastor

The Son of a Ghost

The Son of a Devil

<u>Savage World Series (Monster Romance)</u>

The Heart of an Ogre

Author's Note

Hey Bookish Babes and Bookworms! This spicy romance novel is a part of an interconnected trilogy, some of the plots carry throughout the other two stories. While this is a standalone, reading books one and three may enhance your reading experience.

Trigger Warnings

TW:

-Religion

-Parental Death

-Cheating & Denial of Sexuality (Not between main characters)

-Light Bondage & use of sex toys

This book is a Spicy Romance Novel and may not be suited for all readers.

Readers Discretion is Advised.

The Son of a Ghost Playlist

OBESSED – BRYON JUANE
THE BOY IS MINE –ARIANA GRANDE
STAY FOR A WHILE – VICTOR RAY
YOU DESERVE IT – LEO WATERS
YES IT IS – LEON THOMAS
ALL MINE – BRENT FAIYAZ

BOOK TWO IN THE SPRINGVILLE TRILOGY

THE SON OF A GHOST

A SPICY ROMANCE NOVEL

BY: AMBER RODRIGUEZ

1. PROLOUGE

DANIEL

6 months Ago

Cancer.

My dad has late-stage prostate cancer and he's been keeping it from me for *years*. I wait for my best friend August to return from dropping his wife off at their house with a beer in my hand.

My dad's always been stubborn, with his religion, his wife, and now this. Four years ago, they could have saved him, but now his body's given up on him. The only family I have left is going to leave me soon. *It's not fair.*

When August returns I hand him a beer and he takes it, cracking it open sitting down beside me. He sighs, probably waiting for me to speak first. I do, telling him about my dad, "He has prostate cancer. He told me like it was no big deal." I pause taking a sip of my beer because the pain, the betrayal, it's overwhelming.

When I speak again my voice cracks, "He's had it for four years. *Four* years, and I never fucking noticed." I take a deep breath, trying desperately to ease the pain in chest. August asks, "Isn't it curable?" I scoff, saying, "Yeah, which is what I told him, but the man didn't want to go through all of that, saying he'd rather die. I guess he meant that literally."

He's selfish. Stubborn and selfish and- I toss back the rest of my beer trying to silence the voice in my head. August does the same and when our glasses are empty, he replies, "Damn that man. I guess his stubbornness runs that deep."

I hand him another as I take a second one for myself, saying, "Tell me about it. Even now, he's acting like nothing is wrong. Refusing to acknowledge it and going about his day like any other."

We tap our glasses before taking a sip and August asks, "So what made him tell you after all this time?" I sigh, "Because now he's in stage four, which is the most aggressive. The cancer spread to his lungs, which is why he went to the doctors in the first place. He was complaining about chest pains." We sit in silence redigesting the situation. This can't be real.

The pain is too much, and I change the subject bringing up our best friend, Caleb, "Do you still think it was an accident?" August replies in confidence saying, "The evidence proves so. So yeah, I don't think he killed her on purpose."

I laugh half-heartly in disbelief, "Man, I know you and Caleb were kinky sons of bitches, but this? What the fuck is breath play, and how do people get turned on by that shit? We're going to be so fucked if we're wrong."

"Not Daniel McCarter kink shaming. The man known for never fucking the same girl twice. When has Caleb ever held that over your head?" August scolded me but I can hear the playfulness in his voice. I kill my second beer replying, "Yeah, well none of my kinks ever lead to someone's death."

"True," is all August replies. He's silent for before he continues, "Still, I trust our best friend, The evidence proves Caleb killed Kim by accident during a kink session. We've already done our part so as long as his mom does her job correctly, the public won't get involved, turning it into something it's not."

He's right. I'm being salty. I know the situation with Caleb was an accident. I just need something else to focus on. We talk about a little more and eventually sit in silence before August stands to leave, "I better get home. Are you good, man?" I nod, "Good enough."

Knowing I'm not entirely but I know he wants to get back home to his wife. He checks for his keys saying, "Alright, I'll catch you later then. Call me if you need anything."

I wave him off. Watching as he heads to his car and leaves. I take another dep breath trying to wrap my head around everything that's happen in the last twenty-four hours. How will I survive this?

2. Welcome to Springville

ELIZABETH

Present

I hate the heat, and I hate driving.

God must hate me because I'm driving in the middle of May's heat to this town called Springville. At least I would be if my car's check engine light didn't come on and now has me stuck roadside. My eyes are tired from crying, and a lump still feels thick in my throat. It's dark out and there's no summer breeze, just thick stale heat.

I sigh, seeing the town sign right before picking up my phone to call my mother but decide against it. I made it here, right? No need to worry her right now, so instead I quickly look up and call the local mechanic shop. Someone answers in two rings his voice raspy, as if just awaking, "McCarter's Mechanics. How can I help you?" It's an older man's voice on the line. "Hi, my car's broken. I mean my car broke down and it's the middle of the night; any chance you can send someone to help me?"

He laughs and the sound of a bed creaking plays in the background, "Don't worry darling, I'll send to the tow on over and have them bring you to the shop? Can you tell me your general location?" I sign in relief, "Yeah, I think I'm just at the town line. Near the Springville welcome sign." I look around, searching for another landmark, "There's also what looks like an abandoned church nearby."

"Okay, I know just where you are, hold on tight!" He hangs up the phone without asking for my name or a call back number. Tears threaten my eyes as if my day couldn't get any worse. I grab my keys praying this is all a fluke and turn the ignition, "Come on Betsy." She makes the worse skidding sound, and I stop. "Dammit!" I yell looking at myself in the mirror.

The darkest shade of brown fills my iris and red stains my outer eyes. Freckles cover my brown skin as my thick thighs fill the seat, sitting on top of my head are my fresh twenty-eight-inch boho braids. "At least my hair is done," I whisper as the sound of the night's creepy crawlers fill the air. The darkness makes the nearby trees feel eerily haunted.

I'm not sure how much time passes when big bright lights spot me from head on, thank God. I check my yellow sundress to make sure there's no stains and grab my phone as I move to stand outside of my car.

I begin to wave the closer it gets, as if I'm not the only car stuck out here at the front of a quiet town. I can see the silhouette of the driver as the truck slows and passes my car to do a U-turn before pulling in front of my vehicle.

A very tall man comes into view, it's too dark to see his features, but his hair looks short, almost moplike, and his voice rings like velvet in the air, "You mind if I take a look under the hood before hooking it up? It might be an easy fix, like a loose wire." I nod, "Yeah no problem." I go to pop the hood as he moves to grab a flashlight before heading to the front of the car.

I watch as he bends over, taking a look inside. My phone pings with a back-to-back text message that I ignore. "Aren't you going to check that?" he asks, not taking his eyes off of my car's intestines. "Nope," I reply, popping the p. I already know who it is, and after what I just saw, he doesn't deserve another lick of my time.

I sigh, *my time*. So much of it *wasted*.

"What's your name?" I ask him to distract myself. "The names Daniel, Daniel McCarter." I nod, "Nice to meet you, I wish it was under different circumstances." I laugh a little, pointing to my Betsy.

"No worries, it's a pleasure meeting you too," He responds standing up to his full height. I gulp, is he really that tall or am I just short, well I mean I know I'm short so he's probably not that tall, right? He approaches me asking, "When's the last time you had your car serviced?" Nope, he's really freaking tall, 6ft maybe. His figure nearly crowds mine.

I shrug my shoulders, "Last year, I think." He shakes his head laughing in response, "Figures, it looks like the battery and the wires connected to it burnt to a crisp. I'm not sure how long you were driving but it looks like they fried along the way. Let's take it back to the shop and I'll see if we can replace them."

"Okay," I agree, thankful it's not a major fix. I wait as I watch him hook up my Betsy to his tow truck before he asks, "What's your name?" I frown in confusion, I thought we went over introductions already, "What?"

"Well, I told you mine, so don't I get the pleasure of knowing yours," He smiles as he follows me to the passenger side of the cab. "My name's Elizabeth, but people call me Liz," I say as he holds the cab door open for me. If I wasn't so upset from all the events of today, I'd appreciate the gesture. I wait as he closes it behind me and heads over to the driver's side.

Once inside, he asks, "So what brings you to Springville?"

"Family," I say lying, well partially. "Are you moving to town?" he asks. I sigh shaking my head, "I haven't thought that far ahead." I just wanted to drive, and my mind brought me here. Daniel nods, "Ah, so just going with the flow then." I reply, "At the moment that's what it seems."

I look at his hands on the steering wheel, which are bare of any rings. He's about to ask something again but I beat him to it, "You like to talk, don't you?" His smile is bright and inviting, it sends warmth floating in the small cab around us. I sigh, the growing irritation inside me subsides. I should be nice, after everything I've just been through, I could use a friend.

We arrive at the mechanic shop, and I quickly get out of the cab. I watch as he unloads my car into the car garage as he flips on a horribly bright light. I see another car, that has parts sitting on the roof and the hood propped out. The engine is missing and it's practically gutted.

I hope that doesn't have to happen to Betsy. "Glad you made it!" I loosely recognize the voice as the man over the phone. I smile, stepping over to him. He's bald and looks similar to Daniel, only, sicker? At first glance there doesn't seem like anything's wrong, he has age wrinkles in the crisps of his eyes, but the purple hollowing under his eyes is alarming.

He's just as tall as Daniel and his shirt looks like it's covered in grease stains.

I respond, "We did." He walks from a door on the side of the wall, "My name's Scott. I run the shop." He reaches to shake my hand and then points towards Daniel, "That there is my son." He starts walking over to him and I follow behind him, "What's your diagnosis?"

Daniel turns to his father as he meets him in front of the car, they begin talking about Betsy. Now that we're out of the dark, I can see his features clearly, his hair is actually a reddish orange, and sits at the top of his head like a mop of short curls, The fiery brightness is almost mesmerizing. His face is shaved clean, his eyes are emerald green, his body is thick and clear of any visible tattoos.

His eyes meet mine and I blush. I've been caught staring. He smiles at me, "Hey Lizzy."

"Liz." I correct him.

"Lizzy it is," he says amused, and I don't reply. He can call me whatever he wants if he can fix Betsy. "Do you have a place to crash while you're here? We don't have your battery in stock; I'll have to order it online and I'm not sure when it'll be here."

Great, a new town and I'll be car-less. "My grandmother's place," I say. He nods saying something to his father before turning his attention back to me, "I'll drop you off."

We find ourselves pulling up to the small acre of land my grandmother owns. "Thank you for dropping me off," I say adjusting my duffle bag in my lap as he powers off his car. "No problem, just glad I can help. Here's my number, text me so I can reach you about the car battery when it arrives," he says handing me a white ripped paper with scribbling on it. "Thanks," I say finally getting out of the vehicle.

When I reach the doorstep, my cousin swings the door open, "You were supposed to be here hours ago." I yawn feeling the exhaust from today finally weighing on me, "It's nice to see you too

Justin." He rolls his eyes, and I can see he's tired too.

He really must have stayed up all night waiting for me. "Where's your car?" He asks, as he moves so I can walk past him into the house. I shake my head, "I'll tell you in the morning." All I want right now is to sleep.

I wake to the sound of bacon sizzling. As I sit up, my eyes fall on the semi empty spare bedroom I fell asleep in. The smell of bacon fills my noise and pulls me out of bed. I slept in my dress from last night, too tired to change so I move over to my duffle bag and my phone begins to ring, seeing the caller ID I answer it putting it on speaker as I continue to change.

"Liz! What happened? You were supposed to call us when you got there!" both of my sister's voice boom through my cell, we must be on a three-way call. "Sorry, Betsy broke down last night, but I made it to town. I'm actually at grandma's house right now, though I haven't spoken to her yet."

My sister Clementine, who we call Clay, replies first, "Well I'm glad you made it, I can't wait to hear what she says when she sees you." My other sister Suzanne, who we call Suzie, chimes in, "Your lucky mom hasn't found out yet, she would have stopped you before you've left and made you turn back around."

Our parents have a weird obsession with long birth names, so nicknames are pretty popular in my family. I respond pulling out a purple bodycon sundress similar to my yellow one, "Yeah and that's exactly why no one has said anything to her yet, right?"

Both of them are silent so I yell, "Clay! Suzie! You promised! You know how crazy mom is about following the path of religion? She'll freak out if she finds out I left!" Clay sighs, "I know Liz, but Brian came to moms house looking for you, so she knows."

My blood boils at the mention of his name and betrayal washes over me all over again. "He cheated on me, Clay and lied! He *hurt* me; can't you see that? Mom is out her bonkers if she thinks I'm not filling divorce papers." Look, my mom's not a bad person, but I've witnessed firsthand her

THE SON OF A GHOST

allowing my father to do as he pleases, and she never made a fuss about it. That won't be me.

"We hear you sis," Suzie begins. I wiggle into my dress and pop the straps on my shoulders as she continues, "Are you going too at least talk to him? He's been blowing up our phones too, you know." I check my hair as I reply, "Yes, I will talk to him, but I don't want him knowing where I am right now, not until I call a lawyer."

They both agree and a sound from the other side of the bedroom door pulls my attention, "I've got to go, I'll keep in touch. Love you guys." I hang up and take a deep breath moving to exit the room. Right as my hand lands on the door, the memory floods my mind.

"Damn keys," I whisper to myself in the middle of the night fiddling with my house keys. Dropping them, I roll my eyes why is the porch light off? I sigh, bending over on the ground to feel for the keys. I'm not drunk, I'm just clumsy and it doesn't help that my phone is dead. After a few seconds of feeling around I pick up the keys and feel for the lock and the doorknob.

I sigh in relief when I hear the bolt click and push inside. My first thought is to turn on the porch light, so I don't realize the whole house is dark. But I'm not surprised technically I'm still supposed to be at Susie's for game night, but I left early. Brian must be in the room.

I quickly start setting my things down and making my way into the living room. Maybe I cook up a quick meal before bed. "Brian, are you awake?" I call out noticing a flicker of light, which could be the tv. He doesn't respond so I make my way further into the living room calling out to him again, but his name dies in my throat as I see him standing nude over couch. Why is he naked? As I get closer, I notice the rocking motion of his hips. I hear a deep gutted moan coming from him, my heart falls in the pit of my stomach, realizing what's happening in front of me.

Our entire relationship flashes in front of my eyes. From when we teens at the church, to our wedding day. He hasn't even noticed me yet. Bile rises in my throat and tears swell in my eyes. He's…he's cheating on me. I continue into the room, noticing the thick scent of sex in the air.

How could he? Do I confront him? Should I wait for him to see me? Desperate to see over his shoulder, to see the person who clearly has his attention, I quietly enter the room. Is this why he's been skipping out on game night? Nearly standing right beside him, I see the person bent over the couch and it's like clarity and heartbreak sucker punch my gut and I gasp. Finally, he sees me, and he freezes.

I see his world crashing behind his eyes, his mind turning and ghostly shade cover his features, and I wait for an explanation, for an apology, for something, but he doesn't speak. The person bent over in front of him does though, "Why'd you stop?" He looks up, seeing me standing here and embarrassment covers his features. What's worse is, I recognize him. James. Brian met him a few weeks ago at the gym and invited him over for dinner. He sat at my dining room table, and smiled in my face, and for what? James moves to cover his cock. "Brian!" he hisses out and that snaps Brian out of whatever frozen trance he's in. Unbelievable.

He finally speaks saying my name, but you know what, I've seen enough. I put my hand up to stop him from talking and I leave. I head back to the front door grabbing my purse and keys, and I just…leave. *

I take a deep breath, remembering where I am. I feel so fucking stupid. My grip on the doorknob tights as I take another deep breath trying to calm the storm in my head, before I pull open the door.

When I wander into the kitchen, I see pictures from my dad's childhood and even baby pictures of me and my sisters line the walls. My grandmother is pulling homemade biscuits out of the oven. "Morning," she says looking over at me.

She doesn't even look fazed to see me. "Morning Mamma Cathy." She's dressed in a long, red, kimono robe, her grey hair still pinned in pink rollers. She's heavyset but still moving around with ease. Her dark skin matches mine and a sense of warmth that feels like home washes over me.

"You know when people come to this town, they're either hiding, or running away from something," she says arching an eyebrow at me as she cuts off the oven. My mouth waters over the bacon, grits, biscuits and eggs I see on the counter.

"So, which is it, Mrs. Potter?" she questions, recapturing my attention. "It's not Potter anymore, just Stone. Elizabeth Stone," I say shaking my head at the image of that night threating to torment me again. It all makes sense now.

I sigh, answering her, "Running. Brian and I are getting a divorce," She doesn't respond at first and she begins to make a plate, and I take a seat at the table. Then she says, "Took you long enough." My head snaps in her direction, and she continues, "honey, I've been around plenty of men in my lifetime to see the signs. It doesn't surprise me one bit."

She walks over to me setting the plate down in front of me and I say, "I'm not even upset that he's gay, Mamma Cathy. I'm more pissed that he lied to me. He's lying to himself! Did he just marry me to fit the image? Did he ever actually love me at all?"

I turn to her knowing I'm about to say something personal, "I can count on one hand how many times we've had sex." I pause, recounting every time I've ever had to beg my husband to touch me and was unsuccessful. Platonically, we worked well together, but romantically our relationship hardly exists. It makes so much sense now I want to scream.

She takes a seat at the table with me, "Religion will do that to people dear. I blame your parents for raising you all to blindly obedient and not questioning the things around you. Maybe you would have seen it sooner." We've been married for two years, is it possible my own desperation for love has blinded me? What did I do wrong? I shake the thoughts away, finally eating the meal in front of me.

Soon, Justin comes into the kitchen, and I briefly remember the younger him when he used to rock his afro puff. Now, his hair a clean-cut fade, his face looks so much older now, but he looks decent. I roll my eyes at the thought of him pulling all the girls in town. If I can't make friends because of him, I'm going to be so upset.

Our grandmother makes a plate for him too, "Thanks moms, don't forget to make a plate for yourself." She dismisses him with a wave. "So, are you going to join us at the salon today?" Justin asks, beginning to eat his food. He's the only grandkid who calls her moms, since she basically raised him. His mom left him here when he was five years old, and we haven't seen her since. All we know is that her name is Sarah, she had a really bad drug addiction, and we never ever bring her up.

Instead of making herself a plate, Mamma Cathy starts to clean up the kitchen. I nod, "Yes, I want to stop at the lawyer's office beforehand, though." He nods smiling, "Okay good. It'll be nice to have an extra set of hands." He pauses, turning his attention to Mamma Cathy, "Ma! Come on, I'll put the food away, come sit and eat!" I watch as he seems so protective over her.

Though I understand, since our parents moved from Springville, they haven't been back since, only sending the grandkids over for holidays and vacation. Even that stopped after a while. "I am a grown woman, Justin. I do not need you dictating me," she huffs at him although she allows him to guide her to the dining table to eat with us. I get a glimpse at her hands as she reaches for her fork and her skin looks hard as rock, which could only be the evidence of working the salon for so long.

"So have you thought about retirement, Mamma Cathy?" I nonchalantly ask. She glares at me. "Now don't start with that, Elizabeth. Justin has already mentioned it. The answer is no. I am not retiring," She responds with finality in her voice. I look over at Justin who shakes his head, and I can see the disappointment in his face.

My heart aches for him, we aren't super close, but we keep in touch. I know that him staying back to help her is putting a toll on dream of DJing in the city. We eat the rest of breakfast in peace, After I offer to put leftovers away and clean up the kitchen so she can rest before we leave.

I head back to the guest bedroom to grab my cell phone and put my silver hoops in. My mind wanders back to Daniel, and I remember to put his number in my phone. I shoot him a quick text saying;

Me: Hey, It's Liz,

He responds quickly saying;

Daniel: Hi, Lizzy

Me: It's just Liz

Daniel: I like Lizzy more

Me: Fine, if I'm Lizzy, then you're Danny

Daniel: Cools :)

I roll my eyes at the text thread and change his contact name to Danny. Two can play this game. My phone pings with a text from Brian and of course I continue to ignore it. When I leave the house, Justin and Cathy are waiting in his car for me. God, I hope my Betsy gets fixed soon, I'd hate to have to bug them for car rides.

We make it to Pinky's Salon, and I swear it's just as I remember from our childhood. Earthtones of orange, greens, and yellows paint the walls. African fixtures hang near the desk along with the picture of its grand opening. I take a deep breath; it always feels like home here. I can see why she doesn't want to let it go.

As soon as she flips her open sign on, I swear customers start spilling in.

3. She's off limits

DANIEL

It's been two days since Lizzy came to town. Her car battery finally arrived this morning, but I'm out having lunch with August and Caleb, My two best friends.

We're currently sitting at Maxxie's Diner. "I'm glad you guys are finally home. I've been so lost without you," I joke as August waves down a waiter as his sun-tanned skin makes him look a few shades darker.

He and his wife Hazel are finally back in town from their honeymoon. "It's nice to be back," he replies, briefly touching his brown hair; it's short and clean, just how he likes to keep his image.

"Yeah, it's nice to be with the gang again," Caleb chimes in, readjusting his long black locs into a ponytail. It's odd to think he was involved in an accidental murder case, which we agreed not to talk about, six months ago. Though with the help of his mom, Cora, he's back out in the open. People still stare though.

The waiter approaches the table with a smile but when her eyes land on me She frowns, "Daniel." I recognize her as the last girl I picked up at the bar. "Megan," I guess her name trying to match her tone. She looks offended says, "It's Mackenzie!"

Immediately I hear August say, "Oh here we go." While Caleb laughs, "Well you fucked up." I give them both a look before turning back to her. "Right, sorry." I reply, leaning back into my chair. I loosely remember promising to call her back but I never did. She huffs, "What can I get you?" August tells her his order and so does Caleb. When it's my turn to order she shuffles away completely ignoring me and I look dumbfounded after her.

Caleb and August break out in laughter, and I point at August, "I'm eating your fries." He only laughs more saying, "I'm so glad I don't have to deal with that shit anymore."

I mock him, "Oh that's right, you and the Mrs. are six months expecting and happily married. Yeah, you're the *perfect* couple."

He's not laughing anymore, "Yeah well fuck off. Hazel *is* perfect and at least I have someone to call mine."

Caleb rolls his eyes, "Yeah, keep that shit all the way over there." I smile, leaking sarcasm from my voice, "See! We used to share, August. Don't you remember how to share."

His face begins to turn red, and I just know he's picturing either me or Caleb's hands all over his wife. Caleb says, "Alright now, Pastor boy. Breath, don't need you passing out and freaking out the wifey." That seems to pull August from his trance, and he takes a deep breath, shaking his head.

"Look, I don't understand why she's so upset. I might have forgotten her name, but she knew it was just a fuck before I stepped foot in her place. They all do," I say unapologetically. I like sex and just sex. I always make that clear before a hookup.

The waiter comes back with two glasses of water and still she ignores me. "That's just rude," I say reaching for Caleb's water. "Well, it wouldn't be so bad if you didn't treat them like a ghost after fucking them," August says taking a sip of his water. Caleb calls the waiter back to get another one.

"I can't help it; I like having sex with different women. It's an art you know. Everything about making them come is literally art and who am I to deny myself the call of an artist," I say dramatically, and they both shake their heads.

Caleb says, "Look bro I don't know about being married with kids and happily ever after, but even I like a solid relationship. I mean we've shared a girl or two but that's just between us."

I'm just about to respond until I spot those familiar braids across the street, hanging down her back like a waterfall. She's looking into the window of the closed down flower shop. Her white dress hugs her body the same way the yellow one did when I first saw her. I lick my lips.

"Speaking of art," I begin, and they both follow my line of vision. Caleb says, "Who's that?" My next muse, that's who. "That's Liz," I respond watching her ass poke out as she continues to look through the glass.

"Wait a minute, is her name Elizabeth?" August says with his attention on me. My head snaps in his direct, "You know her?"

"I barely met her the other day I took Hazel to the Salon. Hazel and her really hit it off and are probably planning playdates as we speak. She's also Justin's cousin, Daniel. Hell no, she's off limits," he says dismissively. I swear my jaw drops to the floor, "What do you mean she's off limits? I've never had limits before."

"Doesn't matter, she's Hazel's friend and Justin's cousin. I already hate that fucker always eyeing my wife. You think I want to deal with him, if you fuck around and break his cousins' heart? Nope, not happening."

Caleb pats my back, "Sorry Daniel, you're going to have to keep your dick in your pants with this one." Irritated, I shove his arm away and he just laughs. The waiter comes back with their food, and I immediately steal August's plate, popping a fry in my mouth.

August pulls it back swiftly, answering a question Caleb just asked but I drown them out, pulling out my phone.

Me: That dress looks good on you.

I watch her look up and around before responding.

Lizzy: Are you stalking me now?

Me: If that's what you'd like me to do

Lizzy: Aren't you supposed to be updating me about my car?

Me: Car update: Still not running but part delivered

She doesn't respond for a minute or two, so I double text her.

Me: Going to install it later today, want to see if it works?

Lizzy: Sure

I smile, pocketing my phone and interrupting August and Caleb, "Later guys." I might not be able to fuck her, but I can still be around her.

They shout their goodbye as I fish my keys out of my pocket. When I walk outside of Maxxie's Diner I no longer see where Lizzy is but that's okay. I head to my truck quickly turning it on and leaving the lot. I've lived in Springville my whole life, so as I drive on the way to the shop, I recognize almost every face I see.

My windows are rolled down, creating a wind that makes the heat bearable. My mind wanders back to Lizzy and the first night we met. She looked like she'd been crying, her eyes puffy and red. She looked like she needed a friend. Then I got a better look at her in the light of the shop, and I couldn't help but notice her curves. She was beautiful, even in her sadness.

Then she saw my dad and I can tell she noticed his sickness. The grim reminder of that drops the smile from my face and I sigh.

The drive to the shop isn't far and when I walk through the doors, it's quiet. "Dad?" I call out and it's silent at first. I head over to the garage and see Lizzy's car as well as our other customers. I walk into the waiting room and there I hear faints painful grunts coming from the bathroom.

"Dad?" I question knocking on the door. "I'll be out in a minute son," he responds just as I hear the sound of him using the bathroom. He hisses right after whispering, "Dammit!" I step away from the door and wait. When he emerges, he looks bent out of shape; his eyes look hollow and his hands tremble as he dries them with a towel, "You okay dad?" I ask, hating that I know the answer.

"I'm fine son, it just hurt to piss," He clasps my shoulder. "Now uh, what were we working on again," he says walking out into the waiting room. Before I can respond he remembers, "Oh yeah that battery came, shall we install it?" Just as he finishes his sentence, he starts coughing. My eyes widen as I move over to him, "Dad, come on." Still coughing he shakes his head in response. I help him sit in nearby chair and he grits out, "Water."

So, I move to get him a cup of water and when I return to him, his coughing has settled. "This is ridiculous dad, why won't you let them treat you?" I say, handing it to him. He takes a sip, then takes a deep breath before responding, "The cancer is in my lungs, my bladder and my liver. Treatment now will only prolong my suffering."

I sit beside him, "I can't believe you." I shake my head in frustration. Why didn't he fight? Why did he just allow the cancer to take over? It's not fucking fair.

"It's my decision son, if God says this is how I'll end, I have no right to intervene," He responds finally breathing evenly. "That's bullshit and you know it," I say standing. This time I see anger in his face, "Now I understand your upset with me, but it's my right! You don't get to punish me for it!"

He begins coughing again and I immediately feel bad for working him up again. I sigh, "I know. Look you need to rest; I can handle the shop today. Go home, okay?" He looks at me, out of breath as his coughing comes to an end.

He wheezes, "Fine, but you call me if you need anything. Anything at all, you hear me?" He stands pointing at me and I nod, "Yeah, yeah, I will old man. Get out of here."

He smiles at me, his worsening condition so evident in his face it hurts my chest. He begins walking away and I'm not sure I hear him correctly, but he says barely over a whisper, "I'll be seeing you soon, Angie." Hearing her name makes the pain in my chest hurt more. I sigh, he's the only family I have left, he's deteriorating right in front of me and there isn't shit I can do about it.

Shaking the thoughts away, I take a deep breath, moving to grab the package battery. Suddenly I hear the front doorbell ring and as I look up, in steps Lizzy, "Hi." I try smiling back at her, but it feels a little forced, "Hey."

"I uh, saw your dad on the way in. He doesn't look too good," she says warily, continuing her way over to me. "Yeah," I begin. No sense in hiding it, I continue, saying, "He has late-stage prostate cancer." Her face falls a little, "I'm so sorry." I refocus on opening the packaging, "yeah, me too." He's definitely not sorry though.

"Should I come back another time?" she asks, pointing back at the door. Being alone right now doesn't sound so fun, so I try shaking the negative energy around me, "No, it's okay. Want to watch me pop it in?" She smiles sincerely, "Yeah I do."

She puts her purse down in the waiting area and follows me to the garage. Her 1968 Orange Volkswagen beetle comes into view, and it amazes me how she's been keeping it running all the time. It's old as shit and the parts even more so. She stands beside me, still in that white dress, she's wearing silver hoop earrings, and her arms are crossed as she watches me.

I smile too myself, remembering how I caught her staring at me that first night we met. "So, tell me about yourself," I say as I begin to remove the old battery. She laughs, "Well, I think I'm having a midlife crisis." She shakes her head adding, "Though I'm only twenty-five." Same age as me, nice. I reply, "What's making it a crisis?" I pick up a tool to help me loosen the bolts.

She sighs, "My husband, *Ex*-Husband cheated on me. Now I'm in the process of divorce and left everything behind. My clients are probably wondering where their wedding designer is, and all of this now has me questioning my religion." She says a mouthful, but it sounds like she needed to let that out. I finally pull out the old battery and begin to position the new one.

Married, cheated on and lost. Life is funny like that sometimes. "Sounds like you need an escape," I reply. Don't we all. "Yeah," she says moving closer to me, while I continue to install the new battery. "I felt like I had my life all worked out, I mean there were parts that absolutely sucked about my marriage–" She cuts herself off as If her thoughts changed focus, then she continues, "Danny, can I ask a personal question?"

She says my name so innocently it shoots warmth through me, "ask away." She takes a deep breath, "During the length of my marriage, we've only had three times. I've never had sex before outside of my marriage, so I have nothing to compare it to. Is that normal? I mean you're a guy, so is that how it's supposed to be?"

I pause, my eyes widen at her, God who the fuck did she marry, a monk? It doesn't even matter how long they've been married for; She's fucking beautiful, how can someone not want to fuck her every chance they got?

"Not for me no," I answer, resuming the install. She sighs dropping her head before looking up to the ceiling, "I should have known." I'm suddenly hyper aware of how close her body is to mine, and it makes my cock stir. Desperate to keep my promise I change the subject, "So it seems we both grew up in religious households?" I connect the last few wires, my eyes burning to look back at her. She says, "So it seems."

"So will you be at church tomorrow morning?" I ask looking at the clean rage beside her. She follows my line of sight reaching for the towel, "Yeah, I probably will, if my grandmother makes me." She hands the towel to me, our fingers accidentally touching, and I swear I feel a spark from where our fingers meet. My hand jumps from the contact and she smiles sheepishly.

"You want to try and start her?" I say clearing my voice as I clean my hands with the towel. She nods and I drop her car keys in her hand. She heads to the driver's side, and I can't help staring at her ass. It's so big and round, it looks fucking delectable.

She looks delectable. Like a sweet little doll made just for me. I look away as she opens the door and gets in. In moments she is turning the ignition, but it cranks, and she stops.

Well, it's not the battery, but it's good it's replaced. She gets out the car pouting a little, "Please tell me we can try something else. I need Betsy, she's been my pride and joy." Her voice sounds desperate as she makes her way over to stand in front of me, her face barely coming up to my chest, I smile, "don't worry I still have a few tricks up my sleeve. I can run a proper diagnostic." She sighs in frustration as she looks at me and dammit those eyes are like black holes trying to consume my every breath. Big, round and begging.

I notice her face is littered in small dark freckles that span under her left eye, across her nose, and end under her right. I can't help myself as I lift my right hand out to touch her face. I feel that electric pulse again as our skin makes contact and I wonder if she feels it too, because she gasps before leaning into my palm.

I look at her full lips, they're a darker shade than the rest of her skin with the center being a darkish pink. I bite my lip to refrain from biting hers. I take a deep breath, inhaling the sweet scent of mangos. "Danny?" She questions and I know all too well the sound of lust laced in her voice. Blood rushes to my cock.

God dammit, I want to fuck her. I want to fuck her, bite her, find out all the pretty sounds she makes when she comes. "Daniel?" She says again and I realize I haven't responded. I drop my hand, taking a step back, praying she doesn't see what she's just done to me. I turn around grabbing her old battery to take to the back storage, "I uh." I clear my voice, "I'll get started on that diagnosis. I'll see you tomorrow, okay?"

She takes a second to respond, "Okay. See you tomorrow, Danny." I wait, liking the nickname, as I hear her walk away and out of the building before I let out a deep breath. Who the fuck knew keeping a promise would be so hard. I roll my eyes looking down at the brick threatening to rip my jeans. I need to solve this problem, and I know just who to call.

I find myself waiting in the back of Maxxie's diner for Mackenzie's shift to end. After I apologized for forgetting her name, I offered to swing by her place tonight but she all but insisted I hide out in the back storage closet until she could sneak away. Am I being desperate right now, I don't know, not answering that.

After what feels like eternity she opens the door, briefly letting the light shine into the dark room as she pulls out a condom and slips in before it goes pitch black again. She squeaks out in surprise as my hands are on her immediately. Her breasts are big in my palms, and I hum immediately thinking of what Lizzy's might feel like. She moves to kiss me, but I flip her around and push her against the wall.

Normally I'd take my time, usually my main focus is her body and her pleasures. But I don't care about any of that right now, as thoughts of Lizzy cloud my mind. I pull down her work pants and take the condom. Moving too fast to make sure she's even wet first. I grip her ass, which is nowhere near the fullness of Lizzy's, but I can pretend. Is that wrong of me? Yes, yes, it is. Do I care? Fuck no. I have a promise to keep and if this how I have to keep it, so be it.

I quickly put on the condom and Mackenzie gasps as she feels the coolness of the piercing, on the tip of my dick, sliding against her pussy. I move to slide into her, and she moans. I try imaging what Lizzy would feel like around me and my cock throbs. I start a fast ravenous pace, desperate to free my mind of her.

I listen intently to the sounds Mackenzie is making, trying to ignore the images of Lizzy in my mind but it doesn't work. Images of Lizzy's lips, her face, those adorable freckles and round eyes. I groan. Her thick thighs and her beautiful ass, I remember her voice saying my name and that's enough to send me over. I groan, pulling out and spilling into the condom.

After, I pull out and clean up my mess while she catches her breath. I sigh tucking myself away. Even though my dick is satisfied, I feel a wave of doom because I already want to see Lizzy again. I turn Mackenzie back around, dropping to my knees and pushing her legs open. I'm determined to fuck these thoughts away because if I can't, I am so fucked.

4. The Church, The Brunch, & The Lawyer's Office

ELIZABETH

I feel like my head just hit the pillow when my alarm blares from my phone. I groan, reaching over to turn it off. I feel more tired than usual. It's probably because the weight of everything is settling upon me or it's because I stayed up way too late last night masturbating to Danny and his green eyes staring into my soul.

I sit up with a huff. Mamma Cathy said church is at 10:30 a.m. and she wants to leave by 9:45 a.m. I swing my legs out of bed hoping I'm up early enough to beat Justin to the bathroom. I grab my toothbrush and toothpaste, tiptoeing into the hall before quietly knocking on the bathroom door.

After freshening up, and doing other bathroom deeds, I don't feel as tired, as I make my way back to the guest bedroom. All that's left is for me to change into a dress. Entering the room, I close the door and quickly pull a simple black, short-sleeved, dress. It's modest enough for church as it stops just above my knees. I continue my morning rituals by putting my mango shea butter lotion on my arms, legs and face.

I pop in silver stud earrings and a matching necklace and pair it with my simple black flats. By the time I'm ready I see Justin waiting in the living room, cleaned up in a nice black suit and my grandmother in a colorful, long kaftan dress, with a matching headwrap.

The ride to church isn't as long as I thought it would be, and the service begins shortly after we arrive. I can see Hazel sitting up front with the rest of the Forkhill family. Justin, Cathy, and I are sitting in the middle row. I swear I'm not looking for him, but I haven't seen Danny yet either.

"Brothers and sisters," The pastor begins, and I feel Mamma Cathy hand me a hand fan while not taking her eyes off the pastor. I thank her silently and I look over at Justin and I notice his eyes are not on the Pastor at all. His eyes are glued to the back of Hazel's head. I almost roll my eyes. Does he know he looks like a yearning puppy dog?

I refocus on the pastor and soon enough a horrible thick cough starts in the back of the church. The pastor along with most of the church ignores it. I turn my head around and there I see Daniel patting his father's back as Scott covers his mouth with a cloth trying to get a hold of the sudden fit.

Immediately I excuse myself from my seat, making sure not to step on Mamma Cathy's toes as I pass her. I head towards the back where Danny and his dad sit but I pass them, making brief eye contact with Danny. I continue walking out into the hall looking for the water station. Quickly, I fill up a paper cup and try not to spill it as I make my way back into the church.

I squat down beside Scott as I place the cup in his hand. "Here drink this," I whisper as I look over at Daniel and he's staring at me with an unreadable expression. I turn back to Scott, moving my left hand to rub his back until his coughing settles.

When it does, he quietly thanks me, and I stand moving across in front of him to sit next to Danny. I can't imagine what he's going through watching his dad become weaker and weaker before his eyes. As I sit, I immediately grab his left hand with my right, giving it a squeeze, the only way I can quietly show my support. I try to ignore the fire that burns through me, coming from our interlocked fingers as he looks down at our hands. I keep my eyes on Pastor Forkhill the rest of the service.

"Amen," I say along with the rest of the church as Pastor Forkhill closes out with a prayer. Finally, I release my hand from Daniel's as I stand. Everyone gets up to start conversing with one another. "Thank you," Daniel says, turning to face me. I take in his matching three-piece, dark grey tux.

THE SON OF A GHOST

His fiery red hair is in a slick back, and I have to keep from licking my lips. His tie is a little off centered, but he looks so freaking good.

He recaptures my attention saying, "For helping with my father." I smile looking into his eyes, "You don't need to thank me, I'm sure anyone would've helped."

"Son," His dad gets his attention. We both look at him, and he continues, "I'll be right back, I need to use the bathroom." Daniel nods as we both move towards the aisle and before he can say whatever else, we hear his name being called, "Daniel!"

Both of our heads snap to the voice and it's August, Hazel's husband. "Lizzy, have you met one of my best friends, August?" Daniel says as August is giving a look to Daniel that I don't understand but I reply, "Yes of course, it's good to see you again August. Thank you again, for introducing me to that lawyer." Still frowning at Daniel, he nods towards me and under his stare I feel Danny take a step away from me, creating space. That rubs me wrong, but I ignore it and soon I see Hazel emerge from behind August.

A smile lights my face as she comes into view, "Hi Hazel!" She smiles in return, moving to pull me into a hug. Hazel's long curly hair smothers my face, but I don't mind it. Her brown skin is different from mine, with warm undertones that give a golden brown. I'm really glad I met her at the salon, we just clicked. It's so nice having a friend around that doesn't know all my baggage.

"Hi Liz, I just waddled over her to ask if you wanted to come to brunch with us?" She rests her hand on her very pregnant belly and one on her side to support her back. August speaks before I can, "Hazel baby, I don't think she wants to be bothered with our shenanigans."

Hazel immediately responds, "don't be ridiculous." Her eyes land back on me as she says, "It'll be fun!" August look briefly at his wife then at Daniel before saying, "Alright." Hazel smiles. Dismissing myself, I say, "Let me just tell my grandmother and Justin, I won't be riding back with them."

We find ourselves sitting on the outside patio of a small mom and pop café. It's a six-seater table with Hazel and I sitting on the right side end across from each other. August sits in the middle seat, to the right of her.

Caleb, an attractive dark skin man with black dreads, who I learned is also August and Daniel's best friend sits at the other end of the table to the right of August. I don't remember seeing him in the church, but he says he was there. Daniel left to take his father home, before coming along.

Hazel and I are scanning the menu when she gasps, reaching her hand towards her belly. Immediately this alarms August. "Are you okay?" he asks, turning to his wife and she laughs, placing her hand on top of his and pressing the side of her belly. "I'm fine, Everson just kicked me a little harder than normal." He moves to kiss her head but rolls his eyes, "His name is June." She responds, "yeah, we'll see."

I smile to myself at their bickering, I wanted that so bad with Brian but every time I had baby fever, he conveniently worked longer shifts. I sigh; the memory souring my mood. "Something wrong?"

Hazel asks and I look up at her shaking my head. "No, just indecisive. What are you planning to order?" I lie, changing the subject.

"I want a buttery, grilled cheese croissant with pistachio ice cream," she says, like it's the most delicious thing in the world. I laugh, "Okay, well, I hope you enjoy that."

"Daniel! Glad you made it!" Caleb says as my heart rate picks up a beat at the mention of his name. He's smiling as he walks in and takes a seat in the middle chair, next to me. He replies, "Of course I did. You didn't think I'd let you third wheel alone with these two, did you?" He points to Hazel and August.

Hazel says dramatically, "Very funny. ha, ha." As he sits, his thigh brushes slightly against mine, he smiles at the table so I'm not sure if it was intentional or not. "Finally, we can order now," August says, waving down a waiter.

I turn to Daniel asking, "Did your dad make it home okay?" He doesn't even look at me as he responds, "Yup." Okay. I turn my attention to the person that comes to take our order. When it gets to my turn I order the same thing as Hazel, minus the pistachio ice cream. I heard Daniel order something called a Kazookie.

We sit in small conversation, the whole time Daniel's thigh touches mine, but he practically ignores me anytime I try to make conversation with him. By the time our desserts arrive I ask for mine to go and text my cousin for a ride home.

"Are you sure we can give you a ride home?" Hazel asks as she devours her pistachio ice cream. "No, it's okay, I need to stop at the lawyer's office anyway," I respond, grabbing my receipt and to go box just as the waiter sets it down. I don't know what Daniel's issue is and I literally don't have to be around it. I don't even know why it's bothering me so much.

I say goodbye again to the table and Daniel pretends I've said nothing at all. Freaking dickhead. I make my way outside and to make matters worse, Brian is calling my phone again, this time I answer, "What Brian!"

"Divorce papers Liz! You're taking this way out of hand!" He yells through the phone. Damn he got served already? That was fast. Anger ripples through me, "Out of hand, Brian? You cheated on me! You lied to me; you're lying to yourself! You made me believe it was me, all this time I thought something was wrong with me!"

He begs, "I know baby I know, let me explain. Okay, come back home and let's talk about it."

I shake my head trying not to cause a scene, "There's nothing to talk about, and I don't want an explanation. Just tell me one thing. Do you love me? Did you ever love me, Brian?" He takes a deep breath saying, "Liz you know I have love for you baby." I look at the phone bewildered. That's not saying I love you, which tells me he never did.

My voice breaks as I reply, "Yeah, I still have love for you too Brian, but our marriage, it's over. You and I both know it was never going to survive." I pause, as I think I hear him crying on the other end, "No Liz, please don't do this."

I sigh, "I have too, *we* have to. You don't love me Brian, at least not the way I need. Please don't call my phone again, not until the divorce is finalized." I take a deep breath looking around for Justin, "I want you to know, it's okay to be gay Brian." As soon as the words leave my mouth his frustration turns to anger and the last thing I hear him say is not to say that, right before I hang up the phone.

I take another deep breath; I hope he finds peace within himself. I double text Justin asking for his ETA. Suddenly Daniel comes running out the door, "Lizzy!" I roll my eyes, God, will I ever catch a break, "My name is Elizabeth or Liz. As a business, it's awfully unprofessional to give your clients nicknames. Please only contact me if you have an update about my vehicle."

Justin begins to pull up as I pause to breathe. Perfect timing. "Liz," His says my name and the disappointment in his voice almost pulls at my heart strings. *Almost.* I reply getting into Justin's car, "Goodbye Daniel." He jerks hearing his government name fall from my lips. No, maybe I imagined that part. I refuse to look at him as I decide to send Hazel a thanks for brunch text. I don't want to lose the only friend I might have in this town.

I need to figure out what I'm doing here, and I need to contact my clients before they drop me from their service. "I'm glad you asked me to pick you up, I can tell you about it before we get home."

I shake my head not ready for more bad news, "About what?"

He smiles, "Someone offered to buy Pinky's Hair Salon, they want to keep it open and everything." I sigh in relief before excitement takes over, "That's awesome! Wait what do you mean someone?" I watch as the car comes to a stop at a light.

He responds, "The letter came under an anonymous name. I even tried to trace the return label, but it ended at some p.o box number. The initials were C.M.W and there's a phone number and email to respond to if we're interested." Our light turns green, and he takes his foot off the brake.

The initials sound familiar, but I don't ponder it, "I don't know, Justin. It sounds like a scam."

"Okay humor me and say it's not. Moms can retire and I can leave town and pursue my career. She'll have plenty of money to support herself and everything," he says, sounding so hopeful. I really don't want to shoot him down. "Okay I'll bite," I respond.

He smiles as I continue, "Say it is true. You don't hold the papers to Pinky's, only Mamma Cathy does, and we both know she doesn't want to give it up willingly, so how are you going to get her to change her mind?" He stops smiling as he shakes his head, "I have no idea."

"Well, when you get one, let me know." I reply pulling out my phone.

It's been a few days since that Sunday brunch. Daniel has texted me all but three times and none of it relates to my car. I'm currently sitting in my temporary bedroom on the phone with my employee, "Jessica, I know that you love your job, and I love my job, but I can't *do* my job if this venue isn't secured. I need to know if this will be the venue the wedding *will* be held at before I spend over seven plus hours creating multiple mockup venue styles. So go back to that man, shove the deposit down his throat and tell him to call me if he wants to see what a crazy bridezilla sounds like," I huff hanging up the phone, before hearing her response.

Okay so maybe, that was a little rude, but I'm irritated and horny. It doesn't help that even though I've been ignoring Daniel I can't stop thinking about him. I keep trying to masturbate him out of my mind and it doesn't help that my car is b still not running. Maybe I'm going a little stir crazy in this house.

What's worse, Justin brought up the letter to Mamma Cathy, and she nearly caused an argument. I open my laptop, going to my emails to see if I've heard anything from the few apartment places open here in town. I don't want to move back home so for now, Springville it is.

"Hey you ready?" I hear Justin call from the hall. I close my laptop and get off the bed, "yeah coming now!" I grab my cellphone and purse and head out the door.

The drive to the lawyer's office was quiet and the wait in her office was horribly long, but I guess being one of the only lawyers in town means you have a long client list.

"Elizabeth Potter?" Her assistant calls me to the desk. I smile, "It's just Stone." She smiles apologetically, "Mrs. Walker will see you now." I turn to

Justin, and he says, "I'll wait out here." I nod at him before walking through the doors the assistant is pointing at.

When I enter, no ones in the room, so I walk straight to the desk, sitting in the chair across from hers and wait. I see her desk is littered with baby pictures of a little boy. That's sweet. "Miss Stone! It's so good to see you again!" she says, walking in holding an envelope and moves to sit at her desk.

She's a thin, older black women. Her hair looks jet black and is laid in finger curls. Her suit is tan, and her nails are bright red. She looks freaking beautiful. "It's nice seeing you too, Mrs. Walker," I begin. She laughs, "please, call me Cora! Here, I believe this belongs to you!"

My heart drops in anticipation too why lies within this letter. I open it holding my breath, I read through it my heart pounding in my chest until it lands on one solid word. "It's negative," I say, relief flooding through my veins. "My STD and STI test results are negative," I smile, saying it a little louder. I've been silently dying inside, waiting for these results.

I know Brian and I only had sex a handful of times but, you never know. "Congratulations!" she yells, pulling champagne from under her desk. "This for you!" She hands it over and I thank her. Continuing she says, "Now, Mr. Potter has signed and sent back the divorce papers, so the divorce has officially been filed. Since he agreed to all your terms, we don't have to have a meeting with him unless you want to. Other than that, you'll be legally unbound from him in two months!"

Yes! I scream internally. "What about the notion for my name change?" I ask, desperate to remove Potter from my legal name. "Yes, we filled that at the same time, but the process doesn't take as long. By the end of this month, you'll legally be Elizabeth Stone." She says and I smile at her overwhelmed with happiness.

No wonder Cora has so many good reviews. She makes things that can take years, happen in a few months. I'm almost tempted to ask her how, but I don't think I care enough. "Thank you so much Cora!" I reach my hand over her desk to shake her hand.

5. God's Cruel Jokes and Mangos

DANIEL

She's ignoring me and I don't understand why it bothers me so much.

I turn off the shower head after coming to thoughts of her for the second time. I can't shake her voice from my head. The sound of her lustful and angry woven together in my mind like a melody. Her sweet scent of mangos, a promise of a tasty treat.

I shake my head to get the excess water out as I step out of the shower, then wrap my waist in a town. I immediately check my phone to see if she responded to any of my last texts. Which she hasn't.

She's in my blood.

This is ridiculous. Instead, I see a few text messages from Mackenzie, asking me to come over. Yeah, I know I fucked up. I sigh, walking into my bedroom and tossing my phone on my bed. I dress in black basketball shorts and a loose white T-shirt.

After, I call my dad and he takes long to answer, "Hey son." He sounds out of breath. "Hey dad, just letting you know I'm on my way to pick you up." He takes a deep slow breath, "alrighty I'll be ready."

We hang up and I dial August on the way over, he answers in two rings, "I've decided I dislike you. You've been demoted to *second* best friend." He laughs as I hear a bed creak and Hazel giggles in the background, am I on speaker? I drive past Pinky's Salon crossing the heart of town. "What makes you think you held the title of *first* best friend, you goof."

"So rude," I say dramatically. "I've also decided Hazel has been promoted to first best friend," I reply knowing it'll get under his skin. He replies almost instantly, "In your fucking dreams." *Nope,* she's not the one I see when I fall asleep. I laugh, "Guess I'll see her tonight."

August snaps annoyed and maybe a little pissed, "Daniel did you call me to plan your funeral, because I'll happily arrange it for you." I laugh teasing him more, "Woah, there rider, steady now."

"I'm going to hang up," he replies before doing just that. I arrive at my dad's, and I wait five minutes for him to come out, but he doesn't. So, I throw my truck in park, turning off the ignition and heading inside. His front door is unlocked, and I knock as I walk in, "Dad? Are you okay?"

I wait and listen for a moment before I hear, "In here son." I follow his voice to his bedroom, and I refuse to look at the pictures that line the walls as I do. I see him sitting on his bed clutching his side, "I was trying to put my shoes on, but uh." He trails off and I sigh bending down to assist him. Not because it's bothersome but because it's just more evidence of the life fading away from him.

Once both of his shoes are on, I begin to stand but he places both of his hands on my shoulder keeping me in place, "Jesus, don't look so glim Son." I move to look up at him but don't respond. He sighs, "You're looking at me like I'm a ghost. I'm not gone yet." My heart aches because he does look like a damn ghost.

I shrug his hand off of me saying, "Well you're not giving me a choice." His hands fall into his lap as he says, "Regardless of my condition. We're all living on a ticking clock, son. Either way I won't be here forever. You've got to come to terms with that. Promise me Daniel, promise you'll try to find some happiness, after I'm gone." God dammit dad. All these fucking promises. I sigh heavily, saying, "I promise." He smiles at me, while clasping my shoulder, "Good man."

We get to his doctor's appointment and into a room rather quickly. When the doctor comes in, her smile is bright, and I take a seat on the extra room chair. "Afternoon Mr. McCarter, so today we're here to sign the papers for your hospice care plan." She looks over at me to make sure I'm paying attention, "We'll provide you with in home care and a team will be there for you every step of the way. That way the pressure's not all on the family."

I can't help the memory flashing in my mind. The day he told me how my mom died. I couldn't remember her at the time, and it was frustrating because it made me believe my father was in love with a ghost. I remember hearing the rain, and being frustrated when finally, he said she was hit by a drunk driver.

I remember asking him how come it didn't make him mad or sad because I don't remember seeing him cry about it. He said, I believe in our god. God's way is always right, If Angie was meant to join him that day, I have no right to be upset about God collecting his children.

Even now as he sits here, he still holds that mentality. Believing God is right in everything his does. What God does, is play cruel jokes on people. "Daniel?" The doctor pulls my attention from my thoughts. "Hmm," I respond, mentally returning to the present. "We'll need your signature as well, since you're the next of kin. His team will be there first thing tomorrow morning and we also need your written permission for entry into the home." I nod, taking the pen and signing where she points too.

After dropping my dad back off at the house, I swear I was driving home but I find myself pulling up to the mechanic shop. The only positive thing is I did figure out what's wrong with Lizzy's car so I'm praying she'll want to come see if it works in person again.

Me: Car update.

Lizzy: Is Betsy running?

Me: come find out

She takes a moment to respond to my last text, and I hold my breath.

Lizzy: fine

It takes her thirty minutes to arrive and when she walks in, my breath catches in my throat. "So did you fix it?" She walks into the waiting area dressed in an adorable green pencil skirt and bright pink blouse. "Well don't you look professional," I say instead of answering her question. She stops right in front of me, looking up at me like the bravest little doll I've even seen. She crosses her arms saying, "I'm not here to play games Daniel, just tell me if Betsy running now?"

Ouch, I'm *Daniel* again. "I'm sorry about the other day, Lizzy," I say instead of giving her the answers she wants. For some reason it's important to me she knows I wasn't trying to hurt her feelings, I was just trying to keep August off my back. She waits a moment looking up at me and I want to touch those little freckles again. She says, "You were being rude." Her arms still crossed, I reply, "I know. I'm sorry Lizzy." She sighs, her mighty little wall breaking down.

"My dad's hospice care starts tomorrow," I say, feeling the need to tell her. Her face falls and she drops her crossed arms, saying, "Oh Danny, I'm so sorry." She moves even closer to me now, invading my space, "What can I do to help?" She's looking at me with those big round eyes again, so I pull her body flush with mine and she gasps, resting her hands on my arms.

I sigh oddly content with the contact, "Just be here with me, okay?" She nods, and I pull her tighter against me. I don't know why but I rest my head in the swoon of her neck, and she just lets me. I close my eyes, falling more into her comfort, as she moves her hands to run through my hair, petting me with soft slow strokes.

The ache in my chest lightens a little as we stand there, wrapped in each. I take a deep breath and inhale the scent of Mangos. The same scent I smelled on her at church. I relax into her a little more.

After a while she speaks softly saying, "Danny, not to ruin the moment but I have to pee." Almost reluctantly I pull back, saying, "I'll show you where the bathroom is." She follows behind me as I reach the door opening it for her, "I'll be in the garage when you're done." She nods, beginning to close the door, "Okay." I don't wait for the door to shut as I leave.

I wait in the garage standing in front of the closed hood, with her car keys in hand. When she finally comes into view I dangle them in front of me, "Want to start it?" She rolls her eyes but smirks as she walks over to me collecting it. Again, I stare at her figure as she opens the car door and gets in.

When she starts it, it comes to life, and I can see the biggest grin form on her face. She quickly moves to get out of the car, "Oh my god you saved Betsy! Thank you!" My dick jumps from her voice and dammit I want to taste her. She walks up to me ready to pull me into a hug but instead I place my hands on her face and pull her in for a kiss.

Her hands grip on my arms as I bite her lip and she moans into me. I feel the heat of her body surrounding me as the taste of her lips send electric sparks down my spine. My tongue explores her mouth which earns me another moan, and I pull her closer into me, desperate to keep her here.

But then I remember August's voice and the loose words of off limits, and I pull back. She looks bewildered as we're both gasping for air. Lust is evident on her face and in my jeans. I begin, "I can't."

She makes a face of confusion, so I quickly amend, "I can't touch you, Lizzy Doll," I pause, the nickname rolling of my tongue with ease, "but I'm so desperate to see that pretty pussy of yours. Will you touch yourself for me?"

She doesn't respond as her eyes travel down to the bulge in my pants and although she bites her lip, she hesitates, saying, "Are you sure?" I realize though she's not a virgin she's has little to no experience, so I say, "Only if you want to. Your safe with me Lizzy. If you want to stop, we can, okay?"

She's still a moment more before taking a deep breath saying, "Okay Danny, I trust you." Pleasure riddles through me from her words and She begins to pull up her skirt and I watch as she pulls down a black thong down her legs. My dick throbs with anticipation. She backs up to the hood of her car before scooting on top of it and leaning back. Finally, she spreads her legs, and I swear I see heaven.

She's off limits. I have a promise to keep, I'm not sure if I've already broken it but I'll pretend I care enough to try. I shove my hands in my pockets as I say, "Stick two fingers in your mouth, then touch your clit for me Lizzy. Show me how you like to please yourself."

She follows my instructions, and she lets out the faintest moan of please when her fingers touch herself, her eyes never leave mine and I wonder if this is what the angels in the heavens sound like. "Look how beautiful you are. Touching yourself like this just this for me," I say, admiring her and she moans again, my cock throbs watching her juices coat her finger.

I'm suddenly desperate for a taste. I swallow what I can, as she picks up her pace. I watch, taking notes of the movements that make her the loudest.

Is it possible to cum without touching yourself, because I swear, I feel like I'm about to ruin my pants from just watching her. Soon, her motion becomes sloppy as she breathes in quick and short breaths. "That's it, work yourself to an orgasm. Let me hear you."

She whines, "Danny, please-" She gasps and it's too late, her orgasm bursts through her, sending her eyes closed and her legs tightening around her wrist. She moans through the waves, before slumping back on the car. I give her a few moments to come down before I walk up to her. As she opens her eyes, I say, "I'd like to see you do that again." Still hard as a brick, sexual frustration coils through me. I'm so getting August back for denying me this pleasure.

She nods in agreement, probably still clouded by orgasm fog, but I help her sit up and she wiggles her skirt back down, asking, "Do I get to see you come now?"

I smirk, maybe I'll use my cock as insurance to see her again, "next time." She looks at me a moment before saying, "Okay, well thanks for fixing my car. I'm sure you have my email on file for the bill. What was wrong with it, by the way?" She begins to move to the driver side door, and I move to raise the garage door for her to leave, saying, "It was a burnt-out fuse in your fuse box."

She nods, getting into her car, and starting it. Rolling down her window, she says, "Bye Danny." I smile and turn away as she begins to back out, for some reason, I don't want to watch her leave.

When I make it home, I respond to Mackenzie's text, declining the offer and cutting off any future hookups I might have had planned. No matter how bad I want to keep my promise, a fill-in just won't cut it. Lizzy doesn't seem to be leaving my mind anytime soon. I can't get her out of my head, and I think it's because I just need a taste of her.

Yeah, maybe if I just give myself a taste it'll satisfy this growing desire, and I can move on from it. I take a cold shower, and make my way to bed, too tired and irritable for anything else.

It's the first of the month, you know what that means. Bills are due. I'm currently sitting in the mechanic's shop going over all my dad's old paperwork, trying to understand his finances. I always knew I was going to take over the shop eventually, I just hate that it's happening so soon.

I haven't seen Lizzy since I fixed her car, but we've been texting about random things, like her sisters, her job, going on shopping trips with Hazel. I finally put down the pen when the sun's about to set. I'm supposed to be checking on dad, even though he has in-house care, I can't help but feel like shit if I stay away for too long. I close up shop and just as I head out, Lizzy texts me;

Lizzy: Help! My sister has decided to come to town and now I need an excuse to tell her no!

Me: I don't have siblings, but I imagine it can't be that bad. Just tell her you don't want to hang out.

Lizzy: Believe me it is that bad

I don't respond, laughing and she double texts;

Lizzy: It just got worse; she'll be here tomorrow after church. I'm doomed

Me: Can I offer you moral support?

Lizzy: I'd like that.

The next day, I find myself sitting in the back of the church this Sunday morning and it feels so weird to be here without my father. He refuses to come anymore because he thinks he's too much of a distraction. Truthfully, I don't even know why I'm here, I've never taken our religion seriously.

Not after God took my mother from me and left me with no memories of her to look back on too. Now he's taking my father too. Once he's gone that's it. I'll officially be alone in the world.

I guess I could knock someone up and create a family of my own, but I never thought that far. It's like every decision I thought I had years to consider has turned into months, days. It's unfair.

I tune back into my surroundings as I hear Pastor Forkhill's voice boom, "Why me God? We ask ourselves this more often than not. Why do bad things keep happing to *me*?" He looks around the room as he continues, "We know God does mysterious things as he sets his path for you. We *should* be saying thank you, for God only puts his best soldiers through his toughest battles. He only challenges those he knows will come out on the other side!"

I hear a few amens and clapping as he says, "So instead of thinking the mountain too *high*, or the battle too *tough*. Remember to say thank you God! For *you* are one of god's strongest soldiers."

When the service is over, I remain in my seat, trying to allow his words to stick with me. I watch as people greet each other and laugh before saying their goodbyes. When everyone is gone, August walks up to me, "You good, Daniel?" I look up at him still sitting, "Yeah I just need a minute." He pats my shoulder and tells me to take my time. I look back towards the front of church, still wondering what battle God could possibly be preparing me for, When I notice Lizzy emerge from the side hall that leads the bathrooms. Her eyes look red, as she stops in her tracks and turns back down the hall.

I stand, immediately moving to follow her. Why is she crying? What happened to her? As I head towards the side hall, I think maybe she's going back to the bathroom but as I pass the archway, I see the back of her head slipping into a room further down on the right.

I quietly make my way down the hall, passing the bathroom and making it to the door. Opening it slowly, I notice it's the confession room. It's small, with religious paintings hanging on all four walls. There are a few chairs with a makeshift aisle down the center. The room is dimly lit; candles sit in front of a small angelic sculpture in the front of the room.

My eyes finally land on Lizzy, kneeling in front of the sculpture. I hear her sniffle, so I call out softly, "Lizzy?"

Her head snaps in my direction and my heart aches from the sight. Tears stain her cheeks, and she doesn't move as I approach her, "What's wrong? Did something happen?" Her head falls as she squeaks out, "No, I just." She takes a choppy deep breath.

I squat down beside her, grabbing her chin, forcing her to look at me, "You can tell me." She looks into my eyes taking another deep breath as more tears falls, "I'm struggling to see how everything that's happened to me, is all a part of God's plan for me. He gave me someone I thought really loved me. I mean, I gave that man everything Danny, *Everything.*"

The pain in her voice is ripping my insides to shreds, but I refrain from speaking as she continues, "It hurts. It hurts knowing it was all for nothing. It hurts, coming here and feeling like a piece of my faith has been ripped away."

Another tear falls and I move to my knees to pull her into me. She welcomes my embrace, and I inhale that familiar scent of mangos. I say, "I'm so sorry." She cries into me, and I try to comfort her, "I've got you Lizzy, I'm right here." She's heartbroken and the only thing I can do to help, is whisper comforting words, "I'm right here for you."

6. Faith, Pain, & A Little Bit of Pleasure

ELIZABETH

I'm not sure where Danny came from but I'm happy he's here.

Hazel and I have grown pretty close since I've been here, and she's warned me that Daniel's a total frat boy. I believe her, as I'm sure she's only looking out for me, but here he is making me question it, because why is he holding me like his life depends on it.

Why didn't he leave when he saw the tears in my eyes. Yeah, we've been talking casually and hanging out for about a month now, but he could have easily said it's not his problem.

When I'm all cried out, I pull back from him, and pretty sure I've covered him in tears and snot. "Thank you," I say, wiping my face. He smiles, sadness in his eyes, "You don't have to thank me, Lizzy doll. Whenever you need me, I'll be there." He stands, offering me his hand, "Are we still meeting with your sister later?"

I nod as I take his hand. I've grown to love the little nickname he calls me, I know I already have one but this one between us, it feels special.

Of course, he remembers that my sister is coming over. I sigh, the tiredness of bawling my eyes out making me feel droopy, "Honestly, I was hoping she'd cancel." He takes my hand and I'm unsure if he knows that he's lacing our fingers together as he says jokingly, "And miss out on the chance to meet your *dreadful* sister?" We leave the confession room as I reply, "She is dreadful *to me*. In my mother's eyes, she's perfect in every way. Don't get me wrong, I love her but dammit, it sucks living in her shadow sometimes." He laughs, and the sound is like a breath of fresh air.

We continue down the hall as he says, "Awe is my Lizzy doll jealous of her sister?" His response gives me pause, but he's smiling like it's not a big deal. So, I say, "Not jealous, a little envious though." We make it all the way to my car still holding hands when he finally lets my hand go saying, "So where are we meeting?"

I unlock my car door as I respond, "Just at my grandmother's house, I think she's already there and I'm really not in the mood to be out and about." He nods in response saying, "I'll follow you then."

When we make it to Mamma Cathy's and I'm not surprised to see her in the kitchen. Since she attends the church, Sunday is the only day Pinky's Hair Salon is closed. "Hey Mamma Cathy!" I say, Daniel and I stop in front of her. She's currently juicing a lemon for homemade lemonade.

"Hey honey," she says briefly looking up at us, "Hi Daniel, it's nice to properly meet you." She says now cutting a new lemon in two. "It's nice to properly meet you too?" He replies but poses it as a question. I look at him, does he already know her?

As if answering my question, he shrugs his shoulders and shakes his head. "Where's Suzie?" I ask her. She points to the window over the sink, saying, "She's in the backyard, talking on the phone with her husband." I nod at her response and Daniel, and I head to the backyard.

A small garden of veggies and herbal plants are over in the corner as a four chair and a glass table sits in front of us. Suzie's sitting in one chair with her back facing us as. "Hey sis," I say, grabbing her attention. Her skin matches mine and a neat black bob cut frames her face. She dressed in a matching pencil skirt and blazer set. Well put together as always.

As Daniel and I take a seat across from her as she smiles, talking over the phone, "Honey I have to go, I love you." Once she hangs up, her eyes dart between the two of us, "Hey, sis It's good to see you."

I smile, crossing my legs, my dress rises up exposing my thigh, "It's good to see you too. This is Daniel by the way."

She smiles, nodding towards him, "Nice to meet you, Daniel." He smiles back at her repeating similar words.

"So, what brings you to Springville?" I ask, feeling the warmth of Daniel placing his hand on my thigh. He gives me a reassuring squeeze that warms me more than it should, and I clear my throat, "I know you didn't come all this way just to check up on me." She smiles, "I did actually, as your big sis you know it's my responsibility to make sure you are doing okay." Just then my grandmother comes into view with a few glasses of lemonade, "Hey babies, How the heat treating everyone?" We smile at her, and I say, "It's okay, Mamma Cathy."

We thank her as she sets the glasses down along with the pitcher. Dusting her hands she says, "Who would have known a little heartbreak would have my house full of my grandbabies again." Her comment makes me feel a little guilty, but it also pulls at my heartstrings. She continues, "God works in mysterious ways indeed." I take a sip of the lemonade to refrain from rolling my eyes at that comment. I'm sick of hearing about God and his mysteries.

As my grandmother leaves, my sister turns her attention back to us, "Have you found a place yet?" I take another sip of my drink, "Not yet." She shakes her head, "Okay Liz, let me know if you need help. You've been here for a month now, if you need somewhere to stay you know my doors are open to you." Daniel gives my thigh another squeeze, I sigh, "I know Suzie, thank you, it's just a small town, it's a lot harder than I thought it would be."

She nods in understanding before leaving the subject alone. Seeing that I have nothing else to say, Daniel speaks, "So, what do you do for a living? If you don't mind me asking." She raises an eye at the new nickname before responding to him, "Well my husband and I own a couple of small businesses back home, but I want to change our narrative, as we're looking to expand."

He nods, "so you want to expand *here*?" She takes a drink of her lemonade, saying, "We're thinking about it, but we're not sure yet." Her phone begins to ring, and she dismisses herself. She gets up quickly heading back into the house. When she's gone, I finally look down at Daniel's finger now swirling little circles on my thigh. I ask softly, "What are you doing Danny?"

"Touching you," He smirks. That's not what I meant, though I find comfort in the gesture. I look up at him while he's still tracing my thigh, as he says, "So you need a place to stay?"

I rush out the words too quickly, "No, no, I don't *need* a place to stay." I take a deep breath gesturing around me, "I'm fine here. I know I want to stay here in Springville, even after the divorce is finalized, so I've just been looking around." He's still drawing patterns on thigh, taking in my words, "Have you had any luck then." I shake my head, "None, unfortunately."

He smiles looking up at me, "Well, if you need a place to stay, you could move in with me. If you'd like." I look at him baffled as his eyes find mine. Here he is again being kind to me. The man who supposedly worships a woman's body but tramples on their heart. Why is he doing this? Is he just wanting to get in my pants? Is he only saying things he thinks I want to hear so that I'll sleep with him? I mean, I would, but still.

"No, I don't want to intrude. I'll find someplace."

He shrugs his shoulders, pulling away his hand and says, "The offer still stands." I stand, moving from the table and changing the subject, "Thank you again, for being here for me, my sister acts like she's my mother sometimes, it was nice having your support."

He stands as well, now facing me, "I've already said, you don't have to thank me Lizzy." I shrug my shoulders ready to head for the door, when he grabs my arm stopping me, and pulling me into him. The sudden change of movement makes me gasp, before I can say anything his lips are colliding with mine.

It sparks a flame deep in my stomach as I moan against his lips. He tastes so good. I bite his lips, and his arm tightens around me. My pussy pulses with need, and I pull back knowing it won't be satisfied. His eyes blaze with so many unspoken words.

I clear my throat, speaking breathlessly, "What do you want from me, Danny? Please tell me because you're touching me, kissing me, and making me feel things. I need to know what field I'm standing on." His eyes stare at my lips as he responds quietly, "I just want a taste, Lizzy doll."

I take a deep breath, sex, just sex. Okay I can deal with that. I whisper, "So have a taste then." His grip on me tightens as he pulls me back in for a kiss. His lips are more ravenous, demanding even, as his tongue explores mine. I'm hot, breathless and horny as my hands travel down to feel the length of his cock. He groans at the contact, and I whisper, "Take me back to your place."

So that's exactly what he does, we ditch my grandmother's house and I'm fiddling like a crazy woman in the seat of his car. The car ride is quiet, anticipation thick in the air. He rolls his window down and the wind makes his hair dance. I probably should have taken my car for backup, but I'll deal with the consequences of that later.

Soon, Daniel's pulling into the right-side driveway of a duplex apartment. He doesn't say anything as he gets out of the driver's seat and comes around to open the door for me. He's still silent as he holds my hand and guides me up to his doorstep.

I hear him handling his keys before unlocking his door and pulling me through with him.

His home is small; the front door leads straight into the living room which maintains the right side of the house. I look to my left to see an extremely small kitchen, the appliances line the left wall, with limited counter space. Lastly there's a small table with two chairs.

He's silent as I take in the house, it's surprisingly decorated with wooden fixtures, and there's a single picture frame sitting on an end table near a loveseat, which faces a flatscreen on the wall. I begin walking over to it, but he calls to me, "This way Lizzy." Right. I nod, retaking the hand he's holding out for me. We pass a sliding door, which I assume is a hallway closet, then we pass the bathroom with the door open before he pushes into the final door straight ahead.

We enter his bedroom, and I immediately noticed that though the rest of the house is small, his bedroom is big. It's spacious, he has a walk-in closet and a master bathroom. I look at the wooden bed frame that faces the door, holding a California king bed in the center of the room. The corners have doorknob-like fixtures on them. One end table sits to its left with a lamp on it. He's got a brown wooden basket of dirty clothes sticking out, but other than that the room is clean.

I move more into the room, and I hear Daniel shut the door. Soon he's wrapping his arms around waist and whispering into my ear, "Do you trust me?" Truthfully, I haven't known him long enough, but I do. The words come tumbling out of my mouth, "I trust you." His left-hand roams to my breasts before sliding down to the slit of my dress. He says, "Undress for me."

He steps back, turning me around to face him. Does he want a show? I'm not wearing enough layers to make it entertaining, Nervousness and excitement bubbles through me as I move slowly as I reach to pull up the hem of my dress. I pull my dress over my head dropping it to the floor.

My braids sway from being lifted. My yellow panties don't match my white bra, but he doesn't seem bothered as he watches me unclasp it, dropping it to the floor and slipping out of my panties before him.

As I stand there naked, he licks his lips. Immediately I wonder if he's been with a plus size girl before, I'm not ashamed of my body. Not my stomach or my stretch marks, but still I wonder. The way he's looking at me makes me think he's turned on by me. Well, I mean he is; his cock is bulging through his dress pants. "So exquisite," I barely hear him say over my heart loudly beating in my ears.

"Lay back on the bed Lizzy," he commands and again I listen. He watches as I move to crawl to the top of the bed before laying down. I sit up on my elbows as I watch him walk into his closet, I hear the sound of hangers moving, and what sounds like items shuffling a box. Curiosity sends a bolt of thrill through my bones as I wait.

Soon he re-emerges carrying a medium-sized black box in his hands. I notice he's changed into nothing but a pair of black sweatpants. He sets the box down on my right, near my feet. My eyes widen as I watch him pull out black rope, he finally looks at me, grinning, "Still trust me?" I take a moment to nod, because is that a trick question?

THE SON OF A GHOST

He moves toward me, unravelling the rope that's actually two separate ropes. Intrigued, I watch as he begins tying one around my wrist, focusing on the task, quickly knotting it and moving to tie it to the doorknob like part of the bedpost. He's freaking tying me down. Heat creeps up my neck and over my face, do I *like* this? Daniel walks around the bed quickly doing the same to my left wrist.

Once secure, he smiles saying, "There, don't want you interrupting my feast." My breath catches in my throat as his words. I've never seen this dominating side of him, maybe I've had a glimpse, I don't know. He walks back around to the foot of the bed before finally climbing up between my legs.

He starts at my thighs, peppering kissing on my body as he explores. When he reaches my recently trimmed bush, he takes a of deep breath, inhaling me, saying, "Truly divine." He continues his torturous path of sweet kisses and exploration, by the time he reaches my breasts, I'm gasping for air, wet, and dying for relief.

He's taking too damn long. Why won't he just fuck me. "Danny please," I beg, as my arms trapped with the rope, I can't do anything but use my words. It's frustrating and yet I feel my pussy pulse from the restriction. I *do* like this.

He smiles up at me, "Impatient little doll, aren't you?" *YES!*

I roll my eyes tugging on the rope and he laughs, but begins moving back downward, "So beautiful and so impatient, shall I give you some relief?" I whine, "Danny please stop talking and just fuck me!" He shakes his head amused before dropping his head between my thighs in a quick swift motion. I squeal as his tongue takes me by surprise.

His hands grip the underside of my thighs as his tongues explores my pussy. I moan, throwing my head back. He's flicking and licking and- *God, I'm so wet*. I just want him to fill me. "Danny *please,* I want your cock!" He comes up smiling and I see my juices glistening on his lips, "So needy, Lizzy doll." His moves, sucking on my clit and then I feel him stick two fingers inside me. He curls them as he penetrates me and I moan more, that feels so freaking good.

He continues and I feel the familiar high rising inside me. "Danny!" I beg, I need more, so much more. He groans against me as I try rubbing myself against his face. I'm acting desperate and needy, my body's responding in a frenzy. He's gripping me harder, holding me in place as I feel an orgasm bubbling to the surface.

My breaths become quick and shallow, as pleasure blooms in my stomach, all the while his head's still in between my thighs. I feel him stick another finger in and my back arches from the pleasure "So good," I whisper and in a few seconds, I'm coming all over his face and hand, my legs threatening to close around him. "That's it, Lizzy doll," he says finally coming up for air. He's still fingering me through the wave as I moan incoherently.

I slump a little as I come down, my wrist still secured in place above my head, a mild ache forming around them but I don't mind. He pulls his fingers out and looks me dead in the eye as he tastes them. I swear my jaw drops as he hums saying, "Tasty."

I think he's going to untie me, but he leans down and kisses me, making me taste myself on his lips. Then he pulls back and reaches into the box, pulling out a freaking vibrator. My eyes widen at the long white wand with a round head; I watch as he reaches to the top right of me and fishes out a condom.

"What are you doing?" I ask, knowing I'm way too sensitive for that thing. He smiles wickedly as I watch him put the condom on the head of the toy, "I told you I wanted a taste, Lizzy doll. So, we're going to keep going until I get my fill."

I take a deep breath, no way, I usually take at least twenty minutes to cool down before I work up another orgasm. Is this man trying to kill me? Death by orgasm, hilarious.

I say, "Danny I can't, it'll be too much." He clicks on the toy and for some reason the noise makes me jump, "You can. I'm going to make you cum some many times that you say it's too much and you'll beg me to stop, but if you truly want me to stop, call out for mercy and I will. Okay?" Warily I nod, "Okay."

He hovers over me, and I glance down to see his rock-hard cock, imprinting in his sweats. He moves the toy to my chest and I realize it's on a low setting, as it kind of tickles. Then he moves it to my right breast before it touches my nipple, and I hiss. He smiles, "I want to hear your pretty sounds, Lizzy doll. All of them just for me." The wand travels slowly down my stomach all while he's watching my face, my reactions.

When it touches my clit, I cry out a little, he's barely pressing it against me as it creates a pleasurable discomfort. "All your pretty moans, all your pretty cries. They're all mine, Lizzy Doll." He says oddly possessive, but I don't read into it. I can't read into it, it's just sex. He moves it further down along my lips, before bringing it back to my clit and I moan on brink of losing control.

My body is hyper aware of my nerve bundles going off like fire alarms. It feels too good, I think I'm going numb. I moan and squirm underneath him, my eyes brimming with tears, wildly searching for release. He leans down though, kissing me again before whispering above my lips, "Come for me, Lizzy Doll, let me have your release."

I don't know what's hotter, him talking me through this or the fact that he's being so dominant about. In another moment I feel a stronger orgasm burst through me. I cry out as it feels like shards of glass prickling me from the inside out. My body locks up as I'm forced to endure it, pulling on the ropes. A painful kind of pleasure I didn't know could exist.

Finally, when I come down again, he's still hovering over me and I'm out of breath. He peppers my face and neck in soft kisses saying, "You're doing such a good job, Lizzy."

Doing? As in actively? As in this isn't over? "Danny," I begin but his name comes out choppy, probably because I feel tired or maybe dehydrated. "Shh, save your energy doll. I'll go get you some water."

I watch as he leaves me tied up and naked on his bed. He hasn't even fucked me yet and I've had two mind blowing orgasms. Just thinking about his cock has my pussy pulsing with excitement. This is going to be so good, or it's going to end horribly bad.

7. Keeping Promises Has Never Been So Hard

DANIEL

So, I didn't fuck her, but dammit I wanted too. I didn't even pull my cock out until I got every orgasm she'd give me, before reaching the point of passing out. Then I took out my cock, stroked myself on top of her and came over her breasts. After,

I untied her, cleaned her up, and then she passed out within minutes. I didn't fuck her though, so my promise is still intact, right?

After making her come so violently, I didn't have the heart to wake her, so I let her sleep in my bed. I covered her in blankets and pulled her into me so I could fall asleep to her sweet smell of mangos. So, what's with the weird feeling in my chest when I woke up to her already gone.

It was a good thing, right? That I didn't have to give her the morning after *you got to go chat*, but still somehow, I felt weird about her not being there. I know I said a lot of shit that night, did I scare her off? Saying things like *mine* and *belongs to me*, but that's just sex.

I finally drag my ass out of bed and into the shower. I've had a taste of her, and instead of being satisfied, or content, ready to move on to my next muse.

I want more.

I haven't texted her all week though, and she hasn't texted me. I stroke myself to the memory of her screaming my name before I finish washing up. It's Friday, which means I have to go to the shop and finish a replacement on that old GMC that's been sitting there too long. After though, I'm closing early to hang out with my dad.

Really, he just wants to get out of the house. He says the nurses make him feel like an old person. Which I mean he is, but I don't point that out. Once I walk in the shop, I'm not surprised no one is here. It's a small town, the positive; everyone brings their car to you. The negative; When no one's car needs fixing, no one's car needs fixing. I slip my phone in my jeans and switch on the open light. I go through the opening checklist in a breeze.

Within an hour, I'm knuckles deep in replacing that GMC's head gasket. My fingers are black with grime, my shirt's dirty, and I've worked up a sweat. I take a break pausing to wipe my hands with the not so clean towel hanging from my back pocket, before turning to drink from a nearby water bottle.

My eyes land on the spot where Lizzy's car sat, and my dick pulses from the memory of her touching herself for me. Immediately I shrug my shoulders saying fuck it as I pull out my phone ready to break whatever dry spell were in. I call her phone.

"Hi Lizzy," I say as soon as she answers. "Hi Danny," She giggles. I walk over to a nearby stool sitting down on it, "I missed you the other day, you never told me if you made it home." Her voice sounds a little shy as she responds, "Yeah, sorry about that. I didn't want to wake you, and I thought it'd be easier to leave without saying goodbye." My brows knit in confusion, why would she think that? I say, "Right. Well, what have you been up to?"

She sighs, "Nothing much, still apartment hunting, Dealing with clients. Oh! I checked in with my lawyer, everything's been officialized, so by next month I'll be legally single again." She laughs before I can respond, saying, "God that sounds so horrible when I say it out loud."

I already know who her lawyer is and though I don't know the specifics, she gets shit done. I smile, shaking my head as if she can see me, "No it doesn't. That's good news. You must want to celebrate." I hear the sound of a door opening as she replies, "I do actually I was just trying to

THE SON OF A GHOST

convince Justin to go clubbing with me in the next town over." I say, "Sounds like a plan, maybe I should join you." She laughs a little, "Maybe you should. I'll text you the address, yeah?" I have plans, I definitely don't want to bail on my dad, that'll make me feel guilty as shit. I simply say, "We'll see."

"Oh, hold on Danny, Hazel's calling me," she says right before the call drops. I smile, feeling better. I put my phone back in my pocket, before heading to the bathroom with the urge to pee.

I pass the desk and see more pictures of my mother and father and me as a baby. It sucks not being able to remember her, these photos are hard to look at sometimes because of it. I shake the feeling of despair creeping up on me and continue to the restroom.

I finish installing the gasket within another hour. I try to clean up, wash my hands, and close the shop for the day. Before I get to my car, my dad calls my phone, and I answer. "Son are you on your way? You'd said you'd be here by five," His voice is so horse, more fragile even. "Yeah, dad I'm on my way, I'll be there soon."

I stopped at my house to change before picking up my dad, and in no time, we're headed to the heart of town. Today he wants ice cream, so we're getting him ice cream. We approach the little parlor, and I have to help him walk. It hurts to see him like this, but I smile for him. I don't want my frustrations to add to his pain. We sit on the outside patio, he's got a butterscotch ice cream cone with two scoops, and I've got a mango one. After he's consumed what he can he sets the remainder down on a plate and says, "How is Liz doing, you never told me if you fixed up her car?"

"She's doing good, and yeah I did." I respond while still eating the last of my cone.

He starts coughing and I scoot his water on the table towards him, but he just shakes his head until he can stop. When he does, he responds out of breath, "She's a sweetheart, that one." He takes a deep breath, and I nod in agreement. "You know son, you need to start thinking about your future. Settling down." I shake my head as I finish off the cone, "God, Dad, not this again."

"Yes, Daniel. I'm serious, I am dying, and it pains me to think of you being alone when I'm gone," he says touching his chest. "Dad, there are plenty of women in the world to keep me company." He shakes his finger at me, "One of these days that'll no longer be enough son, mark my words." I reach for my water, disagreeing with him, and he continues, "I was just like you, you know. I thought a being in a relationship with just one woman would never satisfy me. Then I met your mother, Angie." Every time he brings her up it makes me feel guilty, I sigh, "I know dad."

He shakes his head, continuing, "She stole my heart before I even realized it, and by the time I did. I almost lost her." He's told me this story a thousand times, but I let him continue anyway, "She was the one for me, Daniel. She was the love of my life. I just want you to be able to find the same and I know she would too." Yep, guilty that's how I feel, I say, "Dad, I'm not going to marry someone just because you want me to."

He sighs again, speaking slowly, "I know, son. All I am saying is, one day you'll find your heart outside of your chest. And when that happens, don't let it get away from you." He starts coughing again, gripping his side, so I say, "Let's get you home."

After dropping off my dad, Caleb asked to hang out, so I head towards his place. Caleb doesn't live in the heart of town like I do. He prefers the isolation of the trees on the edge of town, so when I make it to his house the night covers the sky. I turn off the ignition and decide to text him that I'm here, as I get out of the car.

His house is huge, twice the size of my duplex. I knock before walking in, His house is bare, or should I say simple. He believes that the less clutter around you, the less clutter in the mind. I call out to him as I don't immediately see him when I walk, "Caleb?" As I make my way down the short hall into the living room, he emerges from the threshold of the kitchen with a glass of water. "Right here," he says before taking a sip. I look at him in confusion, "Why are you all dressed up?" He's wearing a black tux with a blood red bowtie and his hair neatly laid in a braid. "I want to go to the black box and since I got kicked out, I can't get in on my own. But you still have your membership right, I can go as your plus one."

I shake my head taking a seat on his living room couch, "Fuck no, I'm not going there." August, Caleb, and I used to go to a BDSM night club pretty often back in the day, but since August got married, he stopped going and Caleb got kicked out after the accident. I only got the membership to hang out with them, but I quickly got bored of it. He sets his glass down nearby and says, "Come on D, I haven't had a pet in a long fucking time, I just want to have a little fun."

Yeah fun, I know what this sadistic fucker really means, "Not happening. We can do something else though, like go to a bar?" He plops down next to me, being dramatic and saying, "Bars aren't fun. Come on, you know I wouldn't be bugging you if August still went, but he stopped going since he's been all happily married and shit."

Before I reply, the idea pops into my mind and I quickly check my phone. Sure enough, Lizzy texted me the address of the club she's at in the next town over. A wide grin spreads across my face as I reply, "We're not going to the black box, but maybe we can still have fun."

I'm dressed in casual jeans and a black polo shirt, while Caleb is dressed like he's sponsoring a movie premiere. The drive to the club is quiet and I find my mind drifting to Lizzy, so I say, "I think I broke my promise, Caleb." When I glance at him, he doesn't look surprise, in fact he laughs saying, "I knew you'd fuck her eventually, we're telling August."

I shake my head, "I didn't fuck her. I made her come, *a lot*, but we didn't fuck." He looks a little confused as he pulls out his phone and says, "Well are you satisfied?" The sound of her moans plays back in my mind, I shake my head again responding, "fuck no."

He's smiling, dialing August number as he replies, "Well that's a first." He puts his phone on speaker, and it rings twice before we hear August's voice, "What." Snappy asshole. Caleb says, "Little D couldn't keep his dick in his pants." We hear August immediately sigh and I restate, "I haven't fucked her yet, but I may have taken her home." Caleb's grinning as August responds, "I should have known you couldn't stay away from the only new girl in town."

Caleb laughs and I agree. She's everywhere, my dad's shop, the church, she's fucking friends with Hazel. I don't think I could stay away from her if I wanted to. I say, "Yeah, well I didn't agree to said promise anyway." Even now she's in my head.

August sounds tired as he responds, "Do what you will, but if Justin comes knocking at my door, I'm kicking your ass. Now I'm going back to bed." He hangs up before either of us can reply.

We arrive at the club, and the parking lot is full. There are all kinds of people outside, smoking, chatting, and drinking. The vibe seems cool. We head inside and immediately my eyes take a moment to adjust to the darkness.

The sound of loud hype music floods my ears along with the buzz of mixed chatter. People are dressed in all kinds of attire and are almost too close together as I have to move walking sideways. "Let's head to the bar!" Caleb yells over the music and I nod, letting him lead the way.

When we make it there, we order two shots of vodka, and I immediately pull out my phone texting Lizzy

Me: Guess who's made it to the club after all.

Caleb grabs my attention saying, "I have a wild hunch on who you might be texting, tell me she's not here." I grin as I reach for the shot glass, "Maybe she is, maybe she isn't." He smiles and we both throw back our shots. As soon as the cool liquid hits my tongue, fire begins to spread through me.

Setting the glass down we both shake our heads and Caleb hollers, "If she is here, there's a high probability you're getting laid tonight, and if that's the case, I need to be out there instead of here, chatting with you." He points out to the crowd as he speaks, and I tease, "Make sure she actually likes being tied up first, *before* you go home with her." He pats my shoulder, "She's gotta like way more than that." With that, he takes off and I check my phone to see Lizzy's response.

Lizzy: Of course you did!
Me: Where are you, I'm all by myself at the bar
Lizzy: I don't know, come and find me :)

I smile at my phone before pocketing it, and head to the dance floor. Looking around, I move through the sea of people, and my eyes finally land on her. She's about five feet away dancing like nobody's watching and it's mesmerizing. She's dressed differently from her everyday sundress. She's wearing an orange schoolgirl skirt, with a white short sleeve crop top. Her braids dance wildly around her as she moves and she's still wearing those hoop earrings. She looks fucking delectable.

When I finally approach her, she opens her eyes, and they look hazy. She's been drinking, no doubt. I lean down to her and say, "Found you." She smiles up at me, "Took you long enough, Justin ditched me two hours ago." She's been here that long?

"Well, I'm glad I saved the day." She laughs, "Dance with me." Before I can protest, she grabs my hand, pulling them around her waist, as she throws her arms around my neck. The music is upbeat, but we find a rhythmic sway. I try not to focus on the feeling of her soft body against mine as we stare eye to eye.

The music changes to something slower so I step back from her, spin her around and pull her back against my chest, she only giggles as my hands slide back around her waist, pressing flat against her stomach. I set my head in the swoon of her neck, inhaling that lovely mango scent and we sway. She begins to whisper something and even though my face is close to hers I don't hear it.

"Something to say doll?" I say into her ear, and she giggles again. Shit, how much has she had to drink? She turns her head enough to say in my ear, "I want you to fuck me, Danny." Her words send a volt of electricity down my spine and blood rushing to my cock, but I say, "I can't. You're intoxicated." She giggles again saying, "So take me home and fuck me in the morning."

I respond, "How do I know you won't leave again?"

"You don't," she says simply and for some reason that's not enough for me. "If I take you home, I'm tying you to the bed just to make sure you don't leave and if somehow you do. I'll find you, bring you back and edge you until your heart breaks for me," I say and maybe the music is making me hear things because I swear, I hear her moan. "How many drinks have you had?" I finally ask, and she giggles holding up her hand. "Only three," she says but she's holding up four fingers.

Fuck it, we're leaving. Better her safe with me than out with someone else. I begin to pull her through the crowd and pull my phone out to quickly tell Caleb I hope he finds a ride, which I have no doubt he will.

Once we step outside, the cool air is refreshing, still holding her hand I hear her protest, "slow down Danny, you're walking too fast." Okay maybe I am. I slow, saying, "Sorry. We're almost to the car."

When we get to it, I open the door for her, and even buckle her in. She laughs saying, "You're being such a gentleman Danny, but don't be soft with me in the morning, okay." I take a deep breath, "You're making it really difficult for me to wait until morning Lizzy." God, I wish she wasn't so drunk right now. I swear I'm really going to tie her to the bed. In a few minutes, I'm slipping into the car, and she lays her seat back a little.

In no time we're headed back to Springville, and Lizzy's quiet as a mouse. Once I get her to my house, she's dancing on the edge of consciousness. I think the car ride made her sleepy. We make it into my bedroom, and she plops down on the right side and gets under the covers.

I take my pants off in a rush leaving my boxers, and just as I take my shirt off, I say, "I'm serious Lizzy, if I wake and you're gone, your ass will pay for it." She mumbles something and I smile, suddenly realizing she's sleeping in my bed for the second time, and we still haven't had sex, what a novelty. Right before I get in bed, I quickly open my end table's bottom drawer and pull out a silver pair of cuffs. Just in case.

8. Who Wakes up Looking This Good?

ELIZABETH

I blink a few times adjusting to the light in the room, I'm lying on my back as I realize I'm not in *my* room. He really took me home, to *his* home. I try to think back if we had sex last night, but I don't believe we did. Plus, I register I still have all my clothes on.

I take a breath and suddenly feel a pounding headache. How much did I drink last night? Hazily, I remember asking him to take me home to fuck me, lord I must have been a mess. I'm glad he didn't take my word for it.

I yaw sitting up and looking over at Daniel who's still sleeping face down. His curls are covering his face, and I get the urge to touch them. I go to lift my right hand and realize there's a freaking hand cuff around it. I lift it more and see that the other cuff is attached to his right arm. "This man," I begin, and he stirs.

He sits up to push his hair back; he blinks a few times, before a heart aching smile forms on his face. Who wakes up looking this good? "I see you didn't leave," he says, smiling. I raise my right arm wiggling it, which pulls on his, "I literally couldn't if I wanted to."

He laughs, reaching for the key on his nightstand with his free arm, "I recall you saying if I took you home, I could fuck you in the morning." The filthiest image of him doing just that flashes in my head but I clear my voice saying, "Maybe shower first, I'm sure I have morning breath." He laughs, quickly unlocking the cuffs around our wrist and we both sit up, "Shower with me." I frown repeating him, "Shower with you?"

"Yeah, so I can make sure you don't leave while I clean up," he says getting out of bed. "I don't have a change of clothes," I protest. He shrugs his shoulders and says, "You can wear something of mine." I shake my head still sitting in his bed and he sighs, "Or I can cuff you to the bed post while you wait."

I toss the blankets off of me, "Okay that is not very gentleman like." He smiles as I follow him into the bathroom saying, "You told me not to be soft, remember."

"Those were words of intoxicated Lizzy." I mumble behind him, definitely remembering those words. I wait for him to start the shower. Snagging his toothpaste and brushing my teeth with finger. He starts to undress as the water heats, which means he just slips off his boxers.

"Is that? Is that a piercing?" I'm staring so obviously at his pierced cock, and he grins, "Wait until you feel it." Immediately heat spreads through me and I gulp at the sight of him, it's not just pierced, but it's hanging so *low*. Oh my god, he's not even hard! I'm doomed, so freaking doomed.

"Are you getting in?" he questions as he steps in, and I realize I'm still fully dressed. I follow after him, taking off my bra and crop top and quickly dropping my skirt and panties. He's seen my body before, so I've got nothing to worry about and yet nervousness racks through.

Thankfully his shower seems spacious enough and I have to raise my leg because it doubles as a tub. He immediately steps back for me to have the water, and I sigh in contentment when the heat hits my skin. I finally turn to face him and watch him as he lathers his washcloth with a newish soap bar, and I can't help my eyes trailing down his body. So wet, so thick and–

"Eyes up here, Lizzy doll," He grins. I roll my eyes and decide to take the washcloth and soap bar from him. He watches me with desire in his eyes. I purposefully put on a show lathering up my breast and rubbing the washcloth between my legs, I glance down right as I see his dick jump. I tease, "You like what you see?"

THE SON OF A GHOST

A moment passes before he's pushing me against the tile wall and kisses me. The sudden action makes me squeal and drop the items. I wrap my arms around his neck as the water hits the side of his back and little droplets bounce onto me.

His mouth dominates mine as he bites my lip, and tongue kisses me. It's like he's trying to consume every drop of me, and I want him to. I feel his cock press hard against me and butterflies erupt in my stomach. I pull back saying, "Danny, I want you inside me, *please*."

He speaks over my lips, "I'm clean and I have condoms. Are you on the pill?" I answer, "Clean as well but not on the pill." I grew up in a religious household who didn't believe in getting in the way of Gods plans, so I didn't bother with it. "Wait here," he says as if I have anywhere to go.

Daniel steps out trailing water behind him, then I hear a drawer open and close before he's back quickly rolling a condom over himself. I've never had sex outside of my marriage before, so I've never worried about using one. Though I guess I should have, considering the outcome. Before I let my mind drift away from me, I eagerly pull him back into the shower. He groans when our lips collide.

The heat still dances around us as he grips his cock, lifts my right leg and angles himself at my entrance. My arms wrap around his neck and right before he slides in, I panic, "Wait!" He pauses and I quickly say, "This is casual sex, right? We're just having sex." I don't know why but it feels all too intimate, and I just need to know we're still on the same field. I can handle casual sex. Right?

"Yes," he says looking into my eyes. He begins rubbing himself against my lips and I feel the pressure of that piercing, he speaks lowly, saying, "I just want a taste." I whisper back, "You've already had a taste." He groans, "I want more." Just as he says those words, he slides into me and dammit, I can feel every inch of him going in. I gasp, closing my eyes briefly, before opening them and finding his. He pushes and pulls until he's completely inside me, until I feel full of him, and I whine a little because he feels *too* big.

I think he's going to take his time as he pulls out slowly but once he does, he groans slamming back into me. "Oh God!" I cry out. His arm is underhooked on my thigh, and he says, "Give me those pretty sounds you make." I moan at his words. Lord, he's pounding so hard into me I'm gripping on his neck trying not to lose my footing. "Danny," I moan, he's so big and it feels so good, a little painful too. He groans, "That's it. It's me that's making you feel good, my cock that's making you full."

"It's too much," I say breathlessly. "You can take it. Look at you taking all of me," he says but my insides disagree. I lean my head against the tile trying not to pass out from the overwhelming sensation and he moves to bite my throat, before kissing it, then biting it again. Holy damn, it's way too much. I don't remember sex feeling this good, this intoxicating.

"Come for me, Lizzy Doll. Play with that clit of yours and come on my cock." His words make me feel like butter as I tentatively move my right hand down to my clit, still gripping his neck with my left.

Once I add my fingers, the combo has an orgasm rising in my gut, "It feels too good. God, it hurts!" I whine. His tongue still dances on my throat as he says, "You feel so fucking perfect. Made just for me, my own little doll." His stroke hasn't wavered, and I can feel myself slipping. His cock feels magnificent, and his words nearly trick me into believing he means them.

A few more seconds and I come losing my footing, but he holds me in place. I cry out his name spasming around him. "So, fucking perfect," I hear him grit out before he's quickly spilling into the condom. He holds me still, resting his head on my shoulder as we catch our breath. "That was hot," I say, once I can breathe again and he agree, pulling out of me. I feel like Jello as I balance myself and I watch him take off the condom, tying it in a knot, and lean out of the shower to toss it in the trash.

I think we're done, but he turns back to me, getting on his knees lifting my leg again. "Danny," I warn, but my gasp cuts me off as his tongue makes contact with my lips. His mouth begins an assault on my pussy. Not again, doesn't he realize you need a cool down moment in between orgasm? "Danny, I can't!" I say holding on to his shoulders.

I realize the water's beginning to run lukewarm. He looks up at me and dammit I want him back inside me, "You can and you better hurry, we still need to finish our shower and don't want the water to run cold." I whine as his tongue finds my clit, and I hold on to him for dear life. Soon he's pulling another orgasm from my soul.

He kisses my inner thighs as I come down. I feel his hand snake around to my ass, as he asks, "Have you fucked back here before?" I take a deep breath flashes of Brian invade my mind. I meant what I said before, I've given everything to him. I take a deep breath before answering, "Yes." He squeezes my ass in responding, saying, "Maybe another day. Let's get you cleaned up."

Finally, he stands kissing me once more, before we both properly wash up with what's left of the warm water. When we get out, I simply collapse on his bed, still a little dazed, "I need to get home, I have none of my necessities here." The towel still covers me as Daniel smiles, beginning to climb over me, "You want to leave so soon?"

A sex demon. That's what he is. He reaches my face hovering over me with his dripping wet curls, and I force myself to look at his eyes, because if I look down, I may not be leaving. I clear my voice, feeling heat light up my body all over again, "Yes, you need to open the shop, right? And I have clients to talk to. If you want me to come back, I can later on." He sighs, leaning down to take a bite of my neck which makes me squeal. He speaks against my skin, saying, "Fine I'll take you home."

"If we're going to be having sex causally, can I ask you not to sleep with anyone while we're sleeping together? Sharing's never really been my thing." I ask.

He lifts his head, still hovering about me, laughs and says, "Fuck, I get it now." I don't understand what he's means and as I'm about to question him, he looks into my eyes, "I wouldn't dream of sharing you, *my* Lizzy Doll." There he goes again, using possessive words. I smile up at him, "Great."

Daniel gets dressed to go to the mechanic shop and I reluctantly put my worn clothes back on. We leave his house, and we listen to a few songs on his playlist that I tease him about. Soon enough we're arriving at my grandmother's house, and he says, "I see your sister's still in town."

I look, following his gaze and see Suzie sitting on the porch with Justin and her husband Carson.

Carson's dressed in a suit; his blue eyes and blond hair bring out the blue in his tie. I swear, just like his wife, they're always dressed to impress.

His car pulls to a stop, and I thank him for the ride before getting out. "Well look who made it home!" Justin says from the porch. "We need to talk, Liz" Suzie says, taking a sip of her coffee.

I nod, "Let me go change." I take my time refreshing up and using my mango scented shea butter lotion all over my body, to make sure I don't get ashy. When I return to the porch, dressed in a tight blue floral sundress, Suzie says, "That's better."

"It's nice to see you again, Liz," Carson greets me right after and I say the same thing to him. Ignoring her previous comment I ask, "I thought you left town Suzie, why are you back?

She replies, "I never left, I got a hotel room and waited for Carson to arrive." Carson and Suzie share the bench on the right, so I join Justin, sitting on the bench closest to the door. I ask, "What are you here to talk about?"

"We all agree, Mamma Cathy's been running Pinky's Hair Salon for generations. Justin's ready to move on to other things but he's worried about her. We all worry about her, it's time her for to retire. We tried writing a letter to her, hoping the zeros would persuade her but as soon as Justin brought it to her attention, she shut him down," she says.

"The anonymous proposal? That was you?" I ask. Carson speaks this time, "Yes, I thought she'd be more interested if she didn't see my name on it, but she's a stubborn woman."

I reply, "Where is she now? You don't think she's hearing all of this." Justin responds this time, "I took her to the hair salon early today." I shake my head, "No, I don't want you turning it into some high fashion, lifeless place."

Suzie quickly shakes her head, "No, we want to keep it. It may need a little remodeling; we love it just as much as you. We'll be the owners but there will be management and proper employees." Okay, that does sound good, I sigh, "She'll never agree."

"Yes, she will," Suzie says, and I look at her in confusion. She continues, "What's the one thing she's always wanted from us?" My eyes widen, knowing the answer immediately, "Babies. Suzie, are you pregnant?" She smiles nodding, "I am." Carson butts in, "We are."

"Oh my god, Suzie! Congrats! Knowing how much mom and her go on about babies, that just might persuade her." I clap in excitement. She thanks me saying, "Yes and I think it'll be the perfect thing for her; she gets to retire and to spend time with the great grandbabies she's always wanted. Justin can stop worrying. We'll move here in town, and the establishment will live on."

I smile, truly thankful that a plan has presented itself. Stubborn as she is, my grandmother has a weak spot for babies. She's been making me fertility herbal teas since Brian and I's wedding, though I never drank it.

"Okay," I say happily and we all cheer. "When will you present it to her?" Justin asks. "Tonight, over dinner, we have the paperwork ready, and I'll tell her about the baby." We cheer again, and I feel a little relief. I really think Springville will be my new home, and to have at least one of my sisters here with me seems like such a blessing.

9. An Addiction & My Best friend's Baby Shower

DANIEL

a month later

It's weird how so much can happen in a month. My dad's significantly worse, Pinky's Hair Salon is having a grand reopening later this week, and Lizzy's now officially divorced. I'm not surprised the divorce happened so quickly, when you have a lawyer like Cora, who can clean up an accidental murder, which we still don't talk about, it's clear she can make anything happen.

Lizzy and I have been constantly hooking up and hanging out, she's even come with me a few times to visit my dad or come to the shop. I keep thinking I'll be satisfied, that the desire to be balls deep in her sweet heaven will be enough and someone else will catch my eye.

Another person to call my muse, but even now, the idea of entertaining someone else has memories of her invading my mind. The sound of her moans invades my head, her comfort invades my soul, the smell of her taunts my lips, and the memory of her around me sends blood to my cock. I've had my taste of Elizabeth Stone, and I'm fucking addicted.

Today, Lizzy and I agreed to go to August and Hazel's baby shower together. Which I'm grateful for since I didn't think to grab a gift besides alcohol. Does that make me a shitty friend? I hope not. So whatever Lizzy brings, I'll just write my name on it too.

THE SON OF A GHOST

She emerges from the store pushing a cart with a few items in When she approaches my truck, I grab a pen from my glove department and step out to help her toss it in the back. "Hi," she says as she begins to toss in three boxes of baby wipes and four boxes of diapers. I ask, "Where are the gifts?" She grabs another box saying, "What do you mean? These *are* the gifts." Confused, I ask, "so no baby clothes?"

"*Everyone* buys baby clothes; she'll appreciate these more." I shrug my shoulders helping her toss in the last few, before I write our names on them. When I finish, she smirks, "If we're pretending you helped me pull seven boxes off the shelf, then I get to drag you to Pinky's reopening, *and* the next time Hazel and August make me third wheel on of their shopping trips. You have to third wheel with me." I laugh, "Isn't shopping supposed to be fun?"

She huffs, "It *is* fun, when it's just us. When she brings August, they can't keep their hands off each other, it's like being around horny teenagers, who push each other's buttons." I laugh again, saying, "Fine, as long as it doesn't interfere with shop hours."

She smiles, "Deal." I ignore the warmth that spreads in my chest at her smile. It's been happening a lot lately, and I swear she knows it does. We move to get in the car and make our way over to the hall that's been rented out for the baby shower.

We are early, but the set up looks nice. Lizzy whispers, "oh my god, this is so beautiful." I guess they did go all out, transforming the large room into a jungle themed paradise. Fake trees act as an archway that we walk under upon entering, with leaves dangling from above.

When we reach the center of the room, six round green cloth covered tables are placed with five chairs on each. There are little elephant place holders in the center of each table. Green, yellow, and orange décor cover the room in different animal designs.

As we reach the front, we see August's parents settling up some more décor, and Lisa smiles as soon as she sees us, "Hi! Daniel." She pulls me into a hug before turning towards Lizzy, "Hi Liz, it's nice to meet you!" Lisa pulls her in for a hug and Lizzy laughs nervously but doesn't refuse her. Yes, Lisa is this handsy with everyone.

"Isn't this exciting! After years of no children around, both of my daughters-in-law's will be having babies!" Lisa says grinning. I know Lizzy doesn't know who she's talking about, but August did tell me his brother wouldn't be here because his wife is due to give birth any day now. "Remind me to congratulate them the next time we see them," I reply and Lisa smiles and nods. Lizzy speaks up, "Where's the gift table, we have a few boxes to bring in."

"Oh yes it's right over there by the blow-up giraffe," Lisa responds pointing and dismissing herself. "Want me to bring them in while you go find August?" Lizzy offers. I shake my head, "No, that'll be too many trips." I grab her hand, lacing her fingers in mine, saying, "Come on." She allows me to tug her back to the car and I pretend not to see the grin she's trying to hide.

Back at the truck, she immediately starts piling the boxes in my hand and I say, "Oh I almost forgot. I have a surprise for you." She sets the second box on top of the first, looking at me in suspicion, "A surprise?"

"Yep." I say, excitedly. She grabs another box, and I continue, "It's to celebrate you officially being a divorcee and all." At this she rolls her eyes, but doesn't say anything so I keep talking, "that means you'll have to come over though, and stay the night." I'm no longer quiet about how much I like it when she sleeps in my bed.

By the third time she woke up cuffed to me, she offered to leave an overnight bag at my house. I don't know what it is but having her in my arms, but it's a comfort I've never known before. An addiction I'm all too happy to consume.

"You go ahead with these, and I'll follow in behind you," she says, gesturing to the building after stacking three boxes high. I nod and carefully go back inside. I walk slowly under the archway, making it to the table without dropping a box, I set them down near the gift table. Still with no sight of August or Hazel, I head back to the entrance only to see Lizzy, walking in with Robert, the town sheriff, another member of the BDSM black box club. They're both holding two boxes and she laughs at something he's saying.

An odd wave of jealousy slicks through my blood. What the fuck is she laughing at and why is he so close to her? As they approach me, he smiles, "Hey Daniel!" It takes everything in me to plaster a smile on my face instead of pushing his ass as far away from her as possible. "Hi," I reply simply as my hands heat. As soon as they set the boxes down, she says, "Thanks for helping me. It's nice meeting you Robert."

No, it's fucking not!

Before he has the chance to respond, I grip her wrist pulling her away saying, "Can I talk to you for a moment?" I keep a grip on her wrist, as I ignore her saying my name in confusion. Walking near the back of the building I pull open the first door that presents itself. Which looks like a storage closet full of spare tables and folding chairs.

If there's a light in here, I don't look for the switch as I pull the door shut and back her into it. Her head is tilted towards me as I feel her breath ghost against my lips, "Danny?" I hear my heart beating in my ears, still upset, with no right to be.

I raise my arms against the door trapping her in between them and before she can speak again,

I lean down, attacking her neck in kisses before biting down on sucking the skin, she squeals, and her arms wrap around me. I'm going to mark her up, so if someone else even looks at her, they'll know she's not up for grabs, she's fucking mine.

As I continue my assault, she moans in my ear, sending blood straight to my cock. I groan, rubbing my hardening cock against her stomach. Finally releasing her skin, I drop to my knees lifting her skirt, and say, "I want you to come for me."

Her hands entangle in my hair as she says breathlessly, "Someone might catch us." Good. Let *Robert* see who's cock she prefers. I rip her pretty laced panties, desperate for a taste of her holy water.

"Danny, those were brand new!" She tries to sound upset but her words come out in breathy moans as I rub a finger against her lips. My cock throbs from how wet she already is, as I say, "I can buy you new ones." Her head falls back against the door as my tongue comes in contact with her pussy. She moans, her grip on my hair tightening as I lap at her like it's the last thing I'll ever do.

It's not long before her thick thighs begin to squeeze me to the verge of suffocation. As long as I die right here between her legs, she can take my air. I don't need it.

She's nearly riding my face, chasing her orgasm and when it comes, she calls out my name, and I tongue fuck her through it.

When she slumps, I don't let a second pass as I stand pulling my dick out, lifting her left leg, and quickly lining my cock to her pussy. Her hands reach to wrap around my neck. "Danny, please tell me you have a condom in your pocket," she whispers, and I groan.

Fuck, I wanted to be inside her so bad, I didn't realize I was about to go in her bare. To make matters worse I don't have one on me.

Still gripping my shaft I ask, "Would you make me stop if I said no?"

I run my pierced tip along her slit, and she shudders saying, "I should, but I won't." I note the hesitation in her voice, so I stop and say, "Tell me what you want Lizzy." Completely still, I wait for a response. I want her to want this just as much as me. I don't want her to regret anything between us.

She takes a deep breath, he words more confident saying, "I want you to fuck me Danny, just like this."

Good enough.

Her words send me into a frenzy, and my cock slips inside her with ease. We both moan as I fill her, and her grip around my neck tightens. I know my girth is stretching her as she cries out in pain, so I say, "That's it, take all of me."

She lets out a whine, "God, I love and hate how big you are." Her pussy clenches around me, adjusting to my size and it makes me groan. "So fucking perfect," I say as I can feel every inch of her around me.

Her pussy hugs my cock like she was made for me. I kiss her as I pull out then sink right back inside of her. She moans into me, sounding like the sweetest melody I'll ever hear in this lifetime. My right-hand finds her clit, as I find a rhythm.

She bites my bottom lip, and I groan, pumping faster. So damn good. I pull back resting my forehead against her as our body heat creates our own

THE SON OF A GHOST

little bubble. I speak barely over a whisper, "You're mine, Lizzy doll. My sweet, little, doll. Made just for me. You are my heaven."

Her pussy clenches around me as she moans and I know another orgasm is working through her body, I continue, "Your body is my temple, your soul my saving grace." I pump into her ravenously, hoping the feeling of my bare cock is sending her down the same spiral she's sending me down. The words flowing from my tongue feel foreign yet true, saying them to her feels not only right but it feels good.

I'm addicted, I'm obsessed, I want her to myself. "Fuck Danny you can't say things like. You can't," Before she finishes her sentence a glass-shattering moan escapes her lips, and her pussy clenches around me, spasming.

She holds on to me trying to catch her breath as she comes down and I feel my own orgasm surfacing. I should pull out. I should *really* pull out, but she feels to fucking good. So wet, so warm, so perfect. I think the only thing that stops me is wanting to see her face when I fill her with my cum.

I pull out, just as a spurt of cum lands on her stomach, I stroke out the rest of it groaning through the pleasure. When I'm spent, I regret not turning on the light, wishing I could see her face, so I move to kiss her instead. I bite her lip, and seek out her tongue, relishing the way she melts under me.

She pulls back to catch her breath and says, "Are we still in the same playing field Danny?" Fuck no, I want her to myself, but that's not what we agreed to, and I don't want to scare her off.

"Yep," I say lying and dammit I wish I could see her face. "I need to clean you up," I sigh looking around, just then the door begins to open, and I pull her into me, so she doesn't fall. August stands there trying to hide a smirk and conveniently toss me a clean towel. Before promptly shutting the door back. Lizzy and I look at one another and burst out laughing.

Once we emerge, there's a lot more people here and I see more gifts have been brought. Lizzy's ripped panties are stuffed in my pocket, and I pray no one heard her, her sounds are only for me.

August and Hazel stand near the front of the room greeting people as they come in. I see a table with a stack of blue and orange cupcakes and notice they've set out a table of finger foods. I hold out my hand towards Lizzy, asking, "You hungry?" She nods and lets me lead her to the table.

I pick from her plate as she piles crackers, cheese, salami, and grapes onto it. She finally pops my hand saying, "If you don't stop picking at my plate, I'll cut your finger off." I laugh stealing another grape anyway, "If you take my finger, then how else will I make you come." She flushes at this response, knowing damn well I don't need my hands.

"Daniel! Glad to see you made it!" I hear August's voice before I see him. I turn to face him saying, "Congrats!" He smiles knowingly at me, but turns to Lizzy who is replacing the food I've taken, "Can I steal him from you Liz?"

She doesn't look up, saying, "Go ahead, feed him while you're at it so he keeps his paws off my plate." This makes August laugh, and I smile a little. We turn away from her and I glance at

Hazel surrounded by Lizzy's grandma, Lisa, and other women from the church.

As we move away from Lizzy, August says, "I have to say, I'm surprised you haven't fucked this up yet, Daniel." Other people mingle around us as he hands me a glass beer bottle before grabbing one for himself from an ice chest nearby.

"Yeah, well…" I begin popping the cap off and we tap our glasses in a brief cheer before taking a sip. Unsure what to reply, I change the subject, "I still can't believe you're going to be a dad."

He smiles, "Neither can I. I'm lucky as shit. You might be lucky too." He doesn't elaborate as we see Caleb strolling in like the oddball he is, I smile, "Always fucking late." August follows my line of sight and raises his glass, "Caleb! I thought you were going to leave me hanging man!"

As Caleb approaches us, August hands him a beer and the first thing Caleb says, "One of you fuckers is glowing and I'm sorry Pastor boy, but it is not you." Fuck is it that obvious I just railed her in the back room? They erupt in laughter, and I take another sip of my beer.

I look back at the food table and I don't see Lizzy. Looking around for her I spot her with Hazel, she's touching her belly and they're making faces. Something constricts in my chest and August steals my attention saying, "God damn, did I look like that?"

Caleb laughs again clasping his hand around August, saying, "Oh no, you looked *worse*." I roll my eyes sipping the rest of my beer saying, "I don't remember teasing you this much about Hazel."

He shakes his head saying, "No you all but threatened to fuck her." Caleb laughs more and I remember the conversation, but that mindset feels so foreign to me now. Thinking of someone else having Lizzy the way I have, is making me see red all over again.

10. A Sex Demon, A Grand Re-opening, & My Ex is Here?

ELIZABETH

I don't think we're on the same playing field. I don't think I was ever on the same playing field and I'm freaking terrified. I don't know when, but somewhere between all the sex, or him just being here for me. No, maybe it's his cock, and his demon sex sorcery, that pulled in me in before I had the chance to breath.

My first casual fling, and I go a dump my heart all into it and I'm so scared. Scared that I had just got out of a marriage and my heart already found someone else to claim, scared I'll give myself to him and I waste another two years because of some secret he's hiding. Dammit it was just supposed to be sex! I haven't even been divorced for a full year yet!

I shake my head trying to re-ground myself. Today is Pinky's grand reopening, under the new ownership of my sister and her husband. Which means all of our family will be here and that means I'll have to face my mother today. I'm actually surprised she's stayed away throughout the whole divorce process, since divorce isn't in her vocabulary.

I take a deep breath, looking at myself in the mirror of my room. The dress I'm wearing hugs me in all the right places, just how I like. It's a white base with small orange flowers scattered all over. The dress is mid-thigh and with short puffy sleeves. I smile. I look like a doll. His doll. Dammit,

I roll my eyes finally adding silver studs in my ears and a silver tear drop necklace.

I can't even be happy he's coming today because being around him means acknowledging my feelings for him. Does he feel the heat that spreads through me every time he touches me, or how I become desperate for his touch when he's too far away? When he says things, I know he doesn't mean, does he know I want them all to be true. I'm hopeless, and scared, but I don't want to give him up.

I haven't seen him since they baby shower, lying about work so I wouldn't have to go to his place. I work on a damn laptop! Though work actually has been keeping me busy this week, he's even told me the shop's been a little busy. Which is good, distance is good.

My phone rings and speak of the sex demon, "Hi Lizzy, you ready?" Daniel's voice flows through the phone and dammit he's not even being seductive, and his voice sends a volt of heat down to the pit of my stomach. "Coming out now," I say, grabbing my purse and leaving the room. He's waiting in his dad's old truck, the paint is peeling, and the engine is loud but it's still running. I slid into the cab, and Daniel smiles, "Don't you look as beautiful as ever, *stranger*." His smile sends butter to knees, and I reply, "Hi, Danny."

I would say the drive is nice as we sit in comfortable silence, but it's not because my body is hyperaware of Daniel's only a foot away from mine, and it's making me antsy. "You okay Lizzy?" Daniel asks. I let out a choppy breath, "I'm fine, just nervous." Kind of, not really. I continue, "I just haven't seen my family since I moved here."

He grins, saying, "Come here." I scoot closer to him, my thigh touching his as I fill the middle seat. He swings his right arm around me, sarcasm dripping from his lips as he says, "You have nothing to be nervous about, I promise I won't leave with them when they realize they absolutely love me." I laugh saying, "Yeah right, they'd drop you off at my door before the days over with once they realize how miserable you are without me."

He smiles brighter, "Well it's a good thing you don't plan to get rid of me anytime soon." I roll my eyes, "Not yet at least." We make it to the heart of town, and he parks a few spaces away from

THE SON OF A GHOST

the entrance of Pinky's Hair Salon. We get out of the car, and he looks me up and down, saying, "Got damn Lizzy, please tell me you're coming over tonight. I still have that surprise for you, you know."

"Of course you do," I respond, heating under his gaze. He holds his arm out for me to loop mine through and I do, saying, "My parents are going to think we're dating, you know. My mother's going to call me a whore because I haven't even been single for a whole year yet."

Suddenly, he's pulling us so we're looping around and walking back towards his car instead of the salon, "We can always go back to my place, or see my dad, you know he wants to see you again anyway Lizzy."

I shake my head, yanking his arm, so we're walking the correct way again, "no, no it's okay." He laughs and I continue, "we can still go see your dad again, if you want me too."

He smiles down at me but doesn't respond as the entrance to the salon comes into view. Immediately, I see my mother, Bethany, and father, Marcus. Next to them, stands Suzie and Carson near the front. Justin, Clay, and Mamma Cathy are standing there as well.

Townspeople gather in front of them cheering, as someone hands Suzie giant scissors to cut the red bow laced through the front door. Crap, did we miss the speeches?

Daniel doesn't let go of my arm as we pad through the crowd who erupts in cheers as the bow drops to the floor. When we get to the front, my face falls, I see there's an extra person standing near my mother.

"Brian?" I say his name, but he doesn't hear me. "Who's that?" Danel asks, speaking into my ear. I reply, "That's my ex-husband." I'm sure I imagine Daniel's grip on my arm tightening as we move to join them up front.

My mom is the first to spot me. "Liz! Oh, baby it's so good to see you!" Her warm welcome startles me a little. "Hi, mom," I say in disbelief, I swore she'd chew me out the first moment she got. My sister Clay pushes her aside, "Hi, Liz!"

My heart squeezes at the sight of my younger sister. She has mid-length starter locs, and her curls are still present on the tips, her black eyes match mine, and as usual she dresses tomboyish with her black cargo pants, and her grey pride t-shirt. I smile saying, "Hi sis, I missed you so much."

Brian continues to stand aside as my father greets me next, "There's my baby girl." He pulls into a hug, and I melt in his arms. I see Justin talking to Carson, but they shoot me a quick wave which I return with a smile.

Finally, my mother clears her throat, eye dashing between Daniel and I. Smiling, I loop my arm through his again, pulling him a little closer to me, "This is Daniel. My-" I stop, unsure what to call him. My current fling? My sex demon? My Boyfriend?

Daniel speaks while I'm still tossing words around in my head saying, "We've recently started dating, we're still figuring out the terminology. Hi, I'm Daniel."

My eyes widen at him, and I can't even disagree as my mother immediately pulls him into a hug saying, "Welcome into the family, Daniel!" I glance at Clay, and she just shrugs her shoulders. Finally, my dad greets him and it's like they steal him away from me, pulling him into the Salon where townspeople are still filling in.

I look at Brian, who's following in after them. Mamma Cathy finally walks up to greet me, "Glad to see you made it baby." She pulls me into a hug, and I feel rooted in place, "What just happened?" Clay laughs at me saying, "I think your boy toy just got hijacked by our parents."

"That's what it feels like," I respond. Mamma Cathy loops her arm through mine saying, "Well you know how this family is about family, your parents are probably asking him when he's going to marry you and when you guys are having babies." Oh Lord. My face heats and I feel like I need to save him before he thinks my family is nuts and no longer wants anything to do with me. I try to tug my arm from Mamma Cathy, but she grips me saying, "he'll be fine dear, if he can handle those two then he'll survive family holidays."

I roll my eyes, with the urge to say we're not really dating on the tip of my tongue. She pats my arm, still holding it as she says, "Now let's have a tour of the new and improved shop, shall we?" Clay's phone rings beside me, and she holds it up saying, "I'll catch up." I frown as Mamma Cathy tugs me inside.

When we walk through the doors, I'm taken aback. It really looks like a brand-new hair salon. It still has Mamma Cathy's earth tones and décor, but it is completely new. There's a proper register at the front desk. A whole new set of wash stations line the wall. And two new client chairs are alongside Mamma Cathy's main chair.

There's greenery and even a family portrait of Mamma Cathy, her late husband, all of their children and the grandkids. It feels warm and homey, my freaking heart swells. "It's so beautiful," I say and Mamma Cathy nods in agreement. We see people dressed in what looks like new uniforms, giving tours and explaining the new equipment.

I never thought I'd see the day Mamma Cathy give this place up, but I am so glad it's still in the family. "I'm still sour my name's not on the paperwork, but I'm glad I could see some life brought back into her," Mamma Cathy says, squeezing my arm a little.

I smile at her, looking around the room, when I spot my parents showing Daniel an African painting, that my grandfather gifted Mamma Cathy for one of their early anniversaries. They're smiling and laughing and for some reason the scene pulls at my heartstrings.

His light complexion and fiery red hair standing out in between their dark skin. "Moms" We both turn our heads to see Justin waving at us. She smiles at me, "Lord let me go see what this man wants." I laugh a little as she dismisses herself. My eyes find my parents again.

My father's right hand on Daniel's shoulder and my mom's left arm slightly around his waist. Dammit, he might think they're being too touchy. I start to move towards them, but Brian comes out of nowhere blocking my path. "Hi Liz." He smiles down at me with those dark brown eyes that used to make my knees weak. Now there's only one set of green eyes that haunt my dreams.

"Hi, Brian. I'm surprised to see you here." I notice his light complexion looks recently tanned. His black short hair sits styled neatly on top of his head. "Yeah, I'm actually surprised they invited me. Since we're *divorced* and all," he says the word likes it taste bad. Sighing, I begin to say, "Brian."

He cuts me off saying, "I know I know; I fucked up and it's over now." Good, but that's not what I was going to say. "Have you, spoken to a therapist or something, about how you feel?" I speak quietly and slowly, refraining from straight up asking if he's accepted his sexuality.

Truthfully it is what it is. I know he can't help who he's attracted to and even though I haven't forgiven him for cheating on me, I'd hate for him to keep living in the dark.

Even though he hurt me, I want him to be able to look at himself and be happy. To love whoever he chooses, out loud and unapologetically. Just like my sister, Clay.

"No, I haven't because there's nothing to talk about," He responds quietly, shoving his hands in his pockets and swaying on his feet. I shake my head feeling sorry for him, "Oh, Brian." I want to give him a hug; it must suck living behind a lie because that's what's expected of you. Being raised in a religious household, I can't imagine the pain he feels, pretending to be something he's not and worse, that he feels like he has to ignore it like it's not there.

He can't fake it forever but until he's ready, I'll keep my mouth shut. I keep my hands to myself saying, "Look Brian, I haven't forgiven you, but I don't hate you. I truly hope one day you find happiness." He shrugs saying, "Yeah, maybe." Before quickly walking away. I take a deep breath, watching him as the lingering sadness for him makes my heart hurt a little.

"Lizzy doll, please don't tell me you're watching him walk away longingly." I hear Daniel's voice before I see him and when I turn around to face him, he takes my breath away. I reply, "Of course not. How are my parents? I'm sorry if they are overbearing."

He smiles, his arms reaching for mine, He stares down at our intertwining fingers as he says, "They are great actually. Your father asked what I do for work. I told him I work at the shop, and your mom asks if I was going to propose to you first or knock you up?"

My eyes widen and I gasp, "Oh my god! How embarrassing, I'm sorry my family is a little crazy, I totally understand if you're upset about it, I mean we're not actually dating anyway." I don't know why I can't stop but suddenly I'm rambling, "and for the record I'd never purposely try to trap you into marriage or pregnancy for that matter." I laugh nervously, catching my breath. Still looking down at our hands, he replies, "Yeah, let's not tell them that though."

He finally looks up at me, wrapping his arms around my waist and continuing, "I think I like your mom and definitely don't want her thinking I'm just hooking up with her daughter, especially now that she expects grandbabies from me."

I laugh nervously, hyper aware of his face being so close to mine. His body pressed against mine, heat pools in my thighs, and I nearly whine, this is not the place to be getting horny. He smiles, his voice coming out in a tease, "uh oh, does that turn you on Lizzy doll?"

Daniel's right hand grips my chin, pulling me dangerously close to his lips, "Is my Lizzy Doll getting excited thinking about my cum filling that womb of yours?" God yes, yes, I am. The image of him coming inside of me has my legs tightening and he smiles, catching the movement.

I can feel him hardening against me and I forget all about the public place we're in. I pull him in, kissing his lips, before attacking his bottom lip with my teeth. His hands wander back around my waist. He groans against me but before I can taste more of him, he pulls back, still holding me he says, "I swear to god, you are coming home with me tonight and if somehow you don't, I'll sneak into your grandmother's house and kidnap you from your bed." His dirty words send a thrill down my spine, and I say, "Maybe we can go there now."

He bites his lips, but shakes his head and sighs, "We can't just yet. Your mother also invited me to the dinner after-party. Which means we have to entertain them a little longer, doll." I groan. pulling away from him completely. Being so close to him and not being able to have him right now feels like torture.

He only laughs, discreetly adjusting his pants. At least I'm not the only one affected. I cross my arms, responding, "We go to the dinner party, and I get to be dessert, afterwards." He laughs, holding out his hand for me, "Deal." I smile, hating that I love spending time with this man, as I slip my hand back in his.

Lesbian or not, my grandmother expects all the women to be in the kitchen, so while Clay can't cook anything that can't be microwaved, she's standing in the kitchen washing the greens in the kitchen sink, Mamma Cathy's is making the potato salad, and Suzie's pulling the peach cobbler out of the oven.

I'm supposed to be bringing my dad the marinated tray of ribs, but for some reason I'm stuck in the hallway, watching through the glass window of the door of my dad stand over the barbeque pit talking to Daniel, both a beer in hand.

I can't hear a word they are saying, but they're laughing and talking animatedly. My heart clenches in my chest as I can so easily see him this way at every family gathering. I can see myself being married to him and having his babies. Someone Hazel initially warned me about it in the beginning. Someone who unintentionally stole my heart. I'm scared he doesn't feel the same and I'm scared if he does.

What if I tell him how I feel, we make it official and then he decides this isn't what he wants? What if, like Brian, I am just not enough for him? All the possibilities of this ending badly has me rooted on the spot. So, for now or until someone tells me to move at least, I'll admire what could be just a little longer.

After a few minutes I find my feet and walk outside. My dad smiles at me, "Rib time!" He sets the beer down, grabbing the tray from me and I intentionally don't make eye contact with Daniel in fear he can see the revelations all over my face.

11. My Family is Embarrassing Me & He Loves it

ELIZABETH

When dinner is ready, we're all sitting at the dinner table and Mamma Cathy is overjoyed from having a full house again. Greens, cornbread, ribs, potato salad, BBQ chicken, and baked beans, sit on the table scattered between us. My grandmother and my dad sit at the ends of the table that's fit for ten people.

I'm sitting between Clay, on my left, who's sitting closest to Mamma Cathy, and Daniel on my right, who's sitting between me and my mother. My mother is closest to my dad who's on her right. Justin, Brian, Suzie and Carson are sitting across from us. I don't dwell on the fact that Brian chose the seat directly across from me.

We're all piling out plates, having a light discussion when my mother is asking Suzie if she wants some wine, "I can't have it." She's smiling as she shakes her head and my mom questions her, "Suzie you're not pregnant, are you?" Suzie nods, and my mother burst into a bubble of joy, "Oh! oh my goodness, congratulations! Now just to get your sisters on board."

The table congratulates Suzie, even though most of us already knew and I respond to my mother's comment, "One grandchild isn't enough mom?" She looks over Daniel and me like I've asked the most bogus question, "No Liz, I need at least four." I feel like that was such a random number, but I laugh, unintentionally looking at Daniel as if asking his opinion.

He shrugs shoulders saying, "Well I guess we should get started then." My mouth falls open, but the table only erupts in laughter. Suzie says, "Oh my god, yes we could be bump twins and our babies will be besties!" Clay fake gags beside me, and I groan, hiding my face in my palms. When I look back up Daniel is smirking. I try to focus on eating my food.

"You could have already had a grandchild, you know," Brian says quietly, as he picks at his food. The table falls silent and my mother questions him in confusion, "What did you say Brian?" My jaw drops mid chew, bile rises to my throat, and suddenly my food doesn't taste good. Quickly I'm grabbing a table napkin and spitting out my food.

Daniel looks at me worried and Brian continues, "Liz didn't tell you? She had an abortion, the first few months into our marriage."

I nearly whisper, heartache taking over me, "It was *not* an abortion Brian, and you know it." I try taking a deep breath, but everyone is staring in confusion, so I sigh, continuing, "I had miscarriage at eight weeks."

The table seems to fall further in silence, and my father looks at me, "Is that true Liz?" I feel Daniel's hand move to rest on my right thigh. My heart constricts in my chest as memories flood my mind of the day I found out I was pregnant. The first time I had an ultrasound that I attended alone, because Brian had to work late.

Unable to respond, my father turns to Brian and says, "You need to leave, right now." I can't bear to look up at my sisters, I'm sure they feel betrayed since I tell them everything. Just not this.

"I was just stating facts," Brian begins but Justin yanks back his seat. My father replies, "No, what you did right now was intentionally disrespectful. We asked you to join this trip in hopes you and Liz could still have a friendship even after the divorce, but it is clear that's not what you want." As my father's talking, Justin is literally pulling Brian out of his seat who looks dumb founded.

My eyes are watering, and I hear Suzie's voice from across the table. Still unable to look at anyone, I scoot my chair back saying, "Excuse me."

THE SON OF A GHOST

Quickly I rush into the hallway bathroom, locking myself in and taking a deep breath. It doesn't hurt as much as it did before, I've made my peace with it after all, it's been a whole year, but to have it thrown in my face like that so randomly, just knocked me off my senses. I count three trying to calm my heart rate before I hear a knock at the door.

"Liz?" Suzie's voice is a whisper on the other side, and I shake my head, taking a deep breath before letting her in. When I open the door, Clay is standing behind her with a sad look on her face and I step aside so they can walk in. I shut the door behind them, and I cross my arms leaning against the back of the door as we stand in the small bathroom.

"I'm so sorry Liz," Clay's the first one to speak, stepping up to hug me and I shake my head, "It's fine. It was a long time ago." Not really but you know, figure of speech.

Suzie hugs me next saying, "No it's not fine. Why didn't you say anything?" She pulls back, waiting for a response. I look at her saying, "you remember when we had that family hiking trip planned? Brian was super enthusiastic, dad was packing unnecessary travel gear, and mom kept saying I was glowing." Suzie's jaw tightens.

I continue, "Well obviously none of us knew how difficult the hike really was, and I pushed and pushed to keep up with you guys." I pause, reminding myself that it's not my fault, that I didn't know. I take a deep breath continuing, "I noticed the blood when we're on our way home from the trip. I didn't think much of it at first because I researched that a little bleeding was normal."

Tears swell in my eyes, but I wipe them away, "but then I started cramping really bad on the way home, and insisted Brian take me to the hospital, I just…knew something was wrong."

"I'm so sorry you've been carrying that grief by yourself all this time Liz," Suzie responds, hugging me again. I smile, though my heart still hurts a little, "It's okay sis. I've made my peace with it. I know I can have more babies, when the time comes." After everything that's happened, I'm kind of glad life worked out the way it did.

Clay speaks, "Is that what you're doing with Daniel?" I look at her shaking my head, "I don't know what I'm doing with Danny."

"Nonsense," Suzie says. I smile again, wiping away the wetness on my cheeks and she continues, "I saw the way you were looking at him at the salon." Clay chimes in, "Yeah and how you practically attacked his face." Heat runs to my cheeks, at the fact that we *were* being watched. "Yeah well, he's hot so," I say. "Are you scared?" Suzie asks, unconsciously moving to rub her belly.

"Yes," I reply over a whisper. I take another deep breath, they know all about my casual arrangement with Daniel, but I guess it doesn't feel so casual anymore. "Are you guys still hooking up?" Suzie asks. Clay smirks saying, "Obviously." A soft smile creeps upon my lips and Suzie replies, "Being afraid is a part of life. In every decision you make there's a risk. You risk things going really good *or* bad, but I think you guys are worth the risk and if it goes bad. You'll always have us to fall back on."

I nod and pull them in for a group hug, "God, I love you guys." They respond telling me they love me too. We pull back and Suzie says, "We'll give you a minute to clean up, then come rejoin us for dinner, okay?" I nod and move to open the bathroom door for them. Once they leave, I close it and lean back against it.

In a few seconds, there's another knock at the door and I think one of them might have forgot something, but as I open it, Daniel's waiting on the other side, "Lizzy?" His face is soft, his eyebrows raised, and eyes full of worry. I gesture for him to come inside. He shuts the door behind him, and immediately pulls me into a hug, I relax into him.

"I'm so sorry Lizzy," he says, pulling away to look at me and my heart flutters in my chest from the eye contact. He continues, "Do you want to talk about it?" I shake my head, definitely not wanting to talk about it with him. Not because it's *him*, but because I'll start picturing what a baby Danny would look like, with his green eyes and fiery hair. Which will make me think of having *his* babies. Then I'll wonder whose genes might be stronger, picturing a tiny little dark skin baby with green eyes or a light brown baby with red hair. Is

THE SON OF A GHOST

it possible they'll come out with one green eye and the other dark brown?

See! I'm doing it right now.

I take a deep breath, saying, "No, I'm okay I just needed a minute to breathe." I feel his arms tighten around me and he doesn't look convinced. He repeats, "Lizzy, I'm so sorry." I laugh a little, "You just said that."

"I know, I feel bad."

My left hand reaches up to try smoothing the worry lines on his forehead, "There's no need, Brian was being a dick." I shrug my shoulders, and my fingers move down the side of his face, "He's going through some things right now and chose to be salty. I've made my peace with it."

My right-hand rests upon his chest as he's still trying to search through my soul, "I feel like a dick. We've been having sex all this time, and I haven't thought to ask how you'd feel, if *that* were to happen."

My heart jumps in my chest from his words and I tease, "Are we having the baby talk right now, Mr. McCarter?" He grants me the most dazzling smile, "I guess we are." I look at his chest, too overwhelmed by his eye contact, "Well in that case, we're not married so, religion or not, I've always wanted to be married to the man I bring children into the world with." I wrap my arms around his neck continuing, "I like what we have Danny." I like what we have *a lot*, I like you, no I think I love you and it scares me.

I don't voice those comments, and he replies, "And what is it that we have, doll?" His arms loosen around my waist and move low, over my ass. I reply, "Sex." That's a safe response. "Just sex?" He questions, both his hands gripping my ass. He squeezes and I yelp, "Yes! Lots of it."

"Well, if that's *all* that we have, I better use it then," Before I can respond, he's moving to scoop me up and I gasp a little as he plops me on the bathroom counter. "Danny! We're in my grandmother's bathroom!" He agrees, saying, "I know, let me make you feel better and then we'll go back out." He moves to kneel in between my thighs, and it sends a pulse straight to my core, but I protest, "but I'm fine, we can go back now."

I remember I'm not wearing panties as he begins pulling up my dress saying, "And we will but first, I'm going to make you feel better, which will make me feel better." When he sees I'm bare, a feral gleam shines in his eyes, and he licks his lips like a mad man.

My dress sits up to my waist and he groans, moving in to smell me. His wild actions turn me on. My hands immediately dig into his hair, and I hear him whisper between my thighs, "Just a taste, then we'll go." The vibration from his voice on my skin, has me moaning with need. He finally sticks his tongue out, tasting me softly. The feeling sends a jolt through me, and he hums, "So fucking sweet."

His mouth attacks my clit, and I gasp. He wraps his arms around my thighs, and I lean back, removing my hands from his hair to support myself. Danny slips a finger inside me before he speaks against my lips, "Give me your pretty sounds doll, let me hear how good I make you feel." He's pumping into me, licking me, and it feels so freaking good. I want to give him exactly what he wants, but I don't want to be loud.

When I keep my mouth shut, he nips roughly at my clit, and I jump with a whimper. He growls, stuffing another finger inside, "Your pleasure belongs to me, your moans, your cum, all of you. Don't you agree?" He looks up at me, waiting for a response, still pumping his fingers into me. The feeling and his possessive talk send ripples of heat down my spine and to my core. "Yes," I say breathlessly trying to maintain control.

He smiles, "Good, now give me what I want." He returns his mouth to my pussy, and I finally moan out loud, reaching for his hair again. He hums his approval, and I feel an orgasm pooling in the pit of my stomach.

"Oh, yes," I moan, beginning to rock against him, desperately chasing my orgasm. "Yes baby, please." *Baby?* Shit that came out of nowhere. Danny either doesn't mind or doesn't notice as he continues trying to pull my soul from my body.

Finally, I feel that familiar warmth bubbles to the surface right before it sends me over a cliff. "Oh god. I'm coming, I'm coming," I say breathlessly riding out the wave, and he hums, drinking up all of me. I slump when the high dies down. Danny stands, immediately kissing me, I can taste myself on his lips and his tongue dashes out to lick mine.

He pulls back whispering, "Say it again, Lizzy doll." So, he *did* hear me. "I'm sorry, it was an accident." He ignores me as his hands move to squeeze my thigh, repeating himself, "Say it again, baby." The way he says it feels like the stroke of a cord directly to my clit. I clench around nothing, suddenly desperately wanting him inside me. I speak slowly, "Danny, baby."

As the words leave my lips, a groan erupts from his throat and he moves to kiss my neck, then he says, "I think I want to hear you call me daddy instead." I laugh as he continues leaving wet trails on my neck, "I am *not* calling you that." He bites me and I moan against him. God how am I supposed to give this up. How am I supposed to walk away from him when this is all said and done?

I hear the buckle of his belt coming undone, so I say teasing him, "you said you only wanted a taste." He's quickly shoving down his pants and gripping his cock as he says, "I want more."

"You need a condom for that," I moan, reminding him, knowing we've only had unprotected sex that one time at the baby shower.

He's lining himself up with me, rubbing against my lips and the feeling pulls a desperate moan from me. "No more condoms," he groans, still teasing me. "No more condoms?" I repeat his words breathlessly. I don't know what he's thinking right now, but the way his cock is still rubbing against me, has me withering in anticipation.

"I want to feel you, all of you, from here on out, Lizzy."

I wrap my arms around him, nodding in agreement, as he finally pushes inside of me, causing me to cry out. Every time we have sex, I think I'll adjust to his size and every time I'm deliciously wrong. He inches himself further in while saying, "That's its baby, you can take me."

His grip on my thighs holds me in place as I try to relax to accommodate him. Damn God, for creating this sex demon with such a big dick, it's not fair. "Danny!" I whine feeling stuffed as he sinks balls deep inside me.

He moans pulling out, "So fucking perfect." Then he pushes back inside me, and my eyes squeeze shut as I whine again. He starts a toe-curling pace saying, "Look at you, Lizzy doll, *my* Lizzy

Doll. So perfect." I open my eyes and he's already looking at me.

His hair is beginning to stick around his face as he works up a sweat and his green eyes look dazed, like he's lost in pleasure. Damn this man, I moan into him, and he moves to rest his head on my shoulder as he says, "I can't get enough of you baby."

His words shoot straight to my core as the sound of skin against skin fills the air.

12. A Big Family Doesn't Seem So Bad

ELIZABETH

I try not to think about the smell of sex that's probably radiating off of me when we return to the dinner table. With Brian gone, everyone's chatting up a storm, and Daniel and I slide right back in as if we never left. "So will you and Carson be moving to town, now that you own Pinky's?" My mother asks and Suzie nods. The news is exciting; I move to eat some of my greens, peaking at Daniel who continues to eat his plate as well. "Well now that the table is full again," Mamma Cathy begins. She looks around us saying, "I bought the abandoned flower store near the café."

I stop chewing and swallow looking at her, directly. Before I can speak, Justin says, "Moms, are you serious?" She takes a sip of her lemonade and nods, "I thought I'd lay my cards on the table, since people were spilling beans." I see Suzie shake her head and Clay throws her hands up in defeat, saying "Mamma Cathy, you were supposed to *retire*!"

My parents are sharing looks amongst themselves, but they haven't stopped eating. I finally speak, not wanting this evening to go sour, "If you truly are interested in restoring the flower shop, then I'm happy for you, Mamma Cathy. I'd love to help you clean it up." Daniel's hand finds its way back to my thigh and I turn, smiling at him.

Mamma Cathy responds, "Thank you dear, that means a lot to me." Finally, my mother speaks, "We tried to tell you kids, Mamma Cathy is workaholic, she doesn't know what to do with herself outside of that and her little remedies." I frown, not sure if my mother meant that as an insult or not.

Justin sighs saying, "I tried to help you moms, but I can't do it anymore. I thought you would settle into the house and be set with the funds, but if that's not what you want then I can't wait until your retirement to start living my life."

He pauses, looking at all of us at the table before saying, "I guess since we all have something to spill, since Moms is set, or was. I'm leaving Springville. I'm supposed to jet out in the next few days or so."

Jesus, this dinner party has turned into a confession booth. "Well, I'm glad you're finally chasing your dreams, Justin, I told you I can take care of myself," Mamma Cathy is the first to respond to him. "Congratulations, kid," My dad says simply, and the table follows suit. I put my head in my hands; this is too much. Daniel's going to think my family is a case of nutcrackers.

I peak over at him again and he's smiling, congratulations Justin as well. His plate is empty and he's sipping a glass of lemonade. I put my hands down and lean over whispering to him, "I promise you we're not this dramatic on a regular day." He smiles at me, "Don't worry, I like the dramatics."

After everyone seems to be out of confessions, we finish our meal, and my mother insists on a family game before we leave. I keep begging Daniel to go but I think he's fallen under my family's spell.

We'll all cramp up in Mamma Cathy's living room, where my grandfather's ashes are sitting in an airtight black vase, near a picture of him on a shelf that faces us. "Just one game, Liz, then you guys can scurry off and make all the babies in the world," My mother says, and I roll my eyes, not again with the baby conversation.

I look at my dad, but he throws his hands up and replies, "Hey, don't look at me, it's your mother with grandbaby-fever." He smiles, moving to sit next to Daniel who's all but jumping with excitement to keep the party going.

She dismisses his remark with a hand wave as she finally picks a game and begins explaining the instructions. I shake my head but sit near Daniel anyway it's going to be a long game.

When we finally say our goodbyes, my eyes are so heavy I fight to stay awake as we make it to the cab. When the car starts moving, I whisper, "Would you be mad if I fell asleep right now?" With my eyes getting heavier by the second, I know this car ride is going to put me to sleep. Daniel whispers back, "Go ahead, I'll wake you when we make it home." I don't bother correcting him, too tired to pick a fight over terminology, but he said it like it's my home too.

The next morning, I wake in Daniel's bed, but this time the bed is empty. Where is he? I look down at the spaghetti strap and short set I barely remember putting on last night and rush out of bed. Before I can feel some type of way about being left alone, Danny emerges from the shower with a towel draped around his waist, and water dripping from his hair.

Lord it's too early for this. "Well morning sleepy head," he smiles, running his hand through his wet hair making it slick backwards. I sigh, plopping back down on his bed, "Literally how are you awake right now."

He laughs before heading to his closet, saying, "Because I have to get to the shop, and later today I'm supposed to go see my dad. I was hoping you'd spend the day with me and maybe after, I can still show you that surprise I made for you." My eyes soften a little as I sit up, saying, "Of course I'll go with you, we just have to stop to grab my laptop and things so I can get some work done too."

"Sounds like a plan," he says, his back facing me as he chooses his clothes. I continue, "So you *made* me something?" He smiles, tossing his clothes on the bed beside me then he drops his towel, "I did."

My face heats and I try not to look at him exposing himself to me. I know we've seen each other naked, but I still feel a little shy looking at him. He laughs at my reaction and moves to put his boxers on saying, "Relax, Lizzy." I stand moving to my duffle bag before saying, "So, last night felt like a shit show."

He responds from somewhere behind me saying, "I enjoyed it, I've never seen a family so lively." I pull out a simple dress, finally turning around to see him slipping on a pair of jeans, "Yeah well it feels a little chaotic sometimes."

I quickly throw on the dress, adjusting my hair as he replies, "Dinners were always quiet when I was a kid. Just me and my dad, most of the time we just sat together in front of the tv. So, seeing everyone interacting and enjoying the time together, it was nice, even with the family drama."

I don't respond feeling a little bad. Here I am complaining about my hot mess of a family and Daniel's only ever had his dad. That's it. No screaming siblings, no one trying to take your clothes, or to save you from bullies. Now that I think about it sounds lonely compared to the lively household I grew up in. "I Well, I'm glad you had fun." I finally say and he smiles back at me as he finishes getting dressed.

After, we swing by my grandmother's house, we make it to the shop and there's a couple out front, sitting in a black minivan. As we approach the door the man gets out to greet Daniel, "Good to see you Mr. McCarter." He reaches to shake Daniel's hand as I follow behind them. Daniel responds, "Mark, come on, I told you it's just Daniel, my dad is *Mr. McCarter*." Mark only shrugs in response, "Well you know, formalities."

We all head inside, and I hear Mark telling Daniel about his car needing a front-wheel alignment, as it keeps drifting off to one side. Daniel asks him to wait in the lobby as he does his opening checklist. I decide to take a seat at the front desk and pull open my laptop to catch up on some client reports and paperwork.

Half an hour goes by when Daniel emerges from the door that leads to the car garage, saying, "You look surprisingly delicious sitting at that desk." My eyes widen, looking around to make sure no one heard him. The room is empty.

I look over at him and see he's now covered in dirt, and his hands are covered in grime. His hair is a little disheveled and he's even worked up a sweat. He's filthy, yet he looks so hot. I say, "Yeah well keep your dirty paws on that side of the desk. It's nice and clean over here." He laughs, walking over to me anyway, saying, "I can do that. I'd rather get you filthy in a different kind of way."

My face heats from his comment but he continues, "How's work stuff going?" I look back at my laptop briefly before responding, "It's fine, nothing as exciting as fixing cars though." I don't necessarily hate my job but sometimes it feels unfulfilling.

Danny replies, "Well, it should only take me fifteen more minutes to finish up, then, if you want, you can watch me work on the next customer's car." I smile at him, "Sounds like fun."

Just then, the shop's desk phone rings and I stupidly answer it, when I realized what I've done it's already too late so I say the same thing Scott said to me when I first called, "McCarter's Mechanics, how can I help you?" I look over nervously at Daniel and he's smiling at me.

The voice on the phone sounds like a teenager as panic carries in their voice, saying, "Hi! I refilled my coolant last night and now, this morning the car won't start. I think I need a tow, but I'm sure I poured it in the right place. I'm panicking because I have a job interview, I need to be there in forty minutes!"

I reply, "I'm so sorry to hear that, can you tell me your general location?" I quickly grab a pen and a random piece of paper and scribble the given address. I reply, "Okay no worries, I'll send Daniel over and I'm sure he'll be able to figure it out, okay?"

After a few more responses, I hang up and immediately begin to apologize, "I'm so sorry for answering the phone, I didn't mean to-" Daniel cuts me off laughing, "No worries, Lizzy, you were a natural. So, what did they want?"

I tell him and hand him the paper with the address, He says, "Okay, I'll finish up out here, then I'll head out. Will you be okay here by yourself?" I smile, saying, "As long as I don't have to crawl under anyone's vehicle, I'm sure I'll be fine." He smiles once more and suddenly the front doorbell rings as the woman with Mark walks in, "I'm sorry, I know you're working on the car, but I just need to use the bathroom."

"Of course!" I say, pointing her in the right direction and Daniel dismisses himself. I get back to my laptop droning out the noise around me until I hear Daniel leave. Mark walks in shortly after saying Daniel sent him to the counter to pay and this makes me panic. "I don't know…" I begin. Answering the phone is one thing but I definitely don't know how he processes payments.

THE SON OF A GHOST

I pull out my phone ready to send Daniel a what the heck text, when I see he's typed out a quick how to list. I shake my head at his text but thank him and return my attention to the guest, "I guess I will be ringing you up today." I move slowly making sure to follow the instructions Daniel sent. We complete the transaction, and I decide to reply to some of my client's emails.

Shortly after the doorbell rings again and I look up to see a woman walking in. "Hi!" I immediately greet her, and she smiles. She looks youthful, maybe athletic as I notice her toned arms and legs, she says, "Hi, I just need my oil changed."

"Okay great, Daniel is helping another customer but have a seat and he'll assist you when he can." She nods in agreement before taking a seat and with all this flow of traffic, I wonder how Daniel's been managing this by himself, since his father no longer can."

Forty-five minutes pass when Daniel returns. I head to the garage and see Daniel in the cab by himself with an old baby blue Cadillac hooked up to the back. I watch as he unloads it, and when he finally walks over to me, I asks, "Where's the kid?"

"I took him to his job interview," He replies like it's no big deal. My heart warms at this, "You're so sweet, I think I'm getting a toothache." He laughs and reaches for me, I squeal, as his dirty arms wrap around me, "No you're going to get me dirty!"

He pulls me further into him, saying, "Too late." I giggle looking up at him. I've got to tell him. I have to tell him that I'm so in love with him before my heart plunges further into the depths of his soul.

Anxiety swims through me as I wonder if he'll feel the same, and I jump out of his arms saying, "You have a customer waiting in the lobby." He looks puzzled at me for a moment before we both head to the lobby area.

She tells him what she told me, and I watch as he hands her a form to fill out before asking for the keys to pull the car into the garage.

As promised, I get to sit and watch him do the oil change and even though it's uneventful, I'm having more fun than I should be.

As he works, he lets me answer the phone some more and before I know it, the sun is setting and we're closing up the shop. Well, he's closing up the shop, I'm just watching him run around. When he locks the front door he says, "Come work for me."

"Work for you?" I repeat, my eyebrows reach my hairline. He grins, "Come work *with* me." Still standing outside of the lobby doors I shake my head, and he pulls me into him speaking before I can respond, "It'll be fun, we worked great together today, Lizzy. Plus, I'll get to be around you more."

"You're asking me to change career paths because it'll be fun?" I say unsure. I mean I can see myself here, it seemed easy enough. I definitely won't be working on cars, but I have the clerical experience and interacting with people is easy.

"I won't drop my clients, but we can give it a try."

The biggest grin spreads across his face, "It'll work out, we practically spend a shit of ton of time together as it is. All you have to do is move in with me and it'll be perfect." *This guy*. I tap his chest, amused, "Pump your breaks Danny, working together and living together are two different things."

He shakes his head still determined, "We practically live together *now*, you're over all the time, we're only having sex with each other, but we might as well be married." My heart rate picks up and I laugh nervously, "Earth to Danny, I think you're trying to move at the speed of light. Let's try working together first." I'm not really against it because he's right, we've been spending so much time together we might as well be dating, but that's the problem.

We're not dating. At least not officially. I haven't told him how I feel and if he feels the same, he certainly hasn't voiced it. I take a deep breath, asking, "Danny, are we…are we still on the same playing field."

He's got this expression on his face I can't read yet his smile hasn't disappeared, "Come over tonight and I'll tell you." My heart backflips in my chest. Is that a yes? Are we no longer just friends with benefits? Then my heart plummets to the pit of my stomach. Does he mean no? Are we no longer on the same page because I want something more and he doesn't and now he's just waiting to tell me? God, I think his response only confuses me more or maybe I'm reading too far into it.

"Okay," is the only thing I say out loud. He releases his hold around me, saying, "Let's go."

The drive over to his father's house is quick. We park out front, and I follow Daniel inside. His father's house is beautiful; it's a single story but it looks like it's spacious. The outside of the house is simple, with faded blue panels, rich green grass, and a concrete pathway that leads to the door.

When we step inside, some of the lights are on, but no one's in the front rooms. The inside looks nice; there's a brown pull out sofa couch facing a small tv. There's a wall of picture frames similar to the ones at my grandmother's house, except it's just pictures of Scott, Daniel, and I'm assuming his mother.

Daniel calls out to his father as I follow him down a spacious hallway where more pictures of them hang. I can't help but notice all the photos with all three of them in it, Daniel is no more than three, maybe five years old. I stand right behind Daniel purposely shielding my view as he opens up one of the doors, just in case his father is indecent.

But I hear him yell, "Get that mush out of my face woman! I told you I'm not hungry."

Daniel steps further into the room and I see his father is sitting in his bed, while his nurse is trying to feed him applesauce.

13. With Her

DANIEL

My father looks like a walking corpse.

Well, almost. His face is significantly slimmer than a couple months ago; he looks like he's tired and in pain. "But you need to eat, Mr. McCarter. You haven't eaten all day," The nurse responds. He pushes her away and I shake my head, "Come on dad, why are you giving her a hard time?"

I feel Lizzy following me into the room, but she's quiet as a mouse. My father finally looks my way and smiles, "Finally, you can take me out of this tomb!" He smiles and I roll my eyes at his exaggeration. He begins to sit up when he notices Lizzy beside me, saying, "Well this must be my lucky day! Why hey there darling, haven't seen you in a while." His voice sounds like it's straining with effort.

"Hi, Scott," Lizzy says softly and for some reason she grips my hand. Can she see what I see? Does she feel how I feel? The hopelessness of losing my dad right in front of me. I squeeze her hand as my dad asks the nurse to help him out of bed.

We leave them to it and decide to wait in the living room. I sit on the couch while Lizzy walks over the wall of pictures. A moment passes before she says, "She looks so beautiful." She's standing in front of the picture from my first easter. I hate that I don't have my own memories of her. Not a single one. "I wish I knew her," I say, sitting further back into the couch.

She looks over at me with a sad smile on her face and I continue, "My dad use to tell me stories of how we'd sit at the kitchen table over breakfast and I'd tease her about having a milk mustache every time we drank milk together or how my favorite stuffed animal was a dragon and one time it go so dirty, she had to wash it and I cried the whole wash cycle because I thought she was hurting him."

She moves to sit next to me with that sad smile on her face speaking softly, "Well, it's nice you have memories of her." I shake my head, sighing, "That's the thing, I have memories of her, but they aren't mine. I hear the stories, and it sounds like she was great, but I don't *feel* them."

Lizzy's lips quiver before she scoots closer next to me, wrapping her arms around one of mine, and leaning her head against me. She whispers close to my ear, "One day, if you have kids, you will have every single memory of your kid's entire life. It may not heal you completely, but one day those holes in your heart will fill. You are going to be such a great father one day, Danny, I know it." She gives me a reassuring squeeze as her words hit home. Having kids used to be unfathomable to me, but now I can see them in my future. I can see them in my future, with *her*.

My dad finally emerges from the hall, "Okay! Let's go take a trip around town!" He smiles completely unaware of the shifted energy in the room. Lizzy rises from the couch first responding to him, "Let's do it!" I smile, liking the way she entertains his delusions. He's already told me where we're going today, and it is certainly not all over town.

The nurse tells us to keep an eye on his breathing and any notices of severe pain as we leave. We find ourselves in the cab of my truck, luckily it is spacious, so we have no problem sitting Lizzy in between us while my dad hangs his arm out the window. We drive towards the center of town and Dad starts reminiscing, "See that building there, Liz?" He's pointing to Tony's Hardware store as she responds, "Yes I see it."

He continues as we pass by it quickly, "When I was a boy, that use to be a music store. I could buy all the best vinyl records there for the best deals. Until the police learned they were pirated copies and ran 'em out of town."

"Oh my gosh!" Lizzy responds with laughter in her voice, and I can't help but place my right hand on her thigh. It comforts me. We drive a few

THE SON OF A GHOST

blocks down almost to our destination, passing by all the mom-and-pop stores.

We're passing the abandoned flower shop Lizzy's grandmother bought, when my dad says pointing to it, "That shop there is where I bought Angie her first flower bouquet. It was a fresh bundle of red roses and we were going on our first date to the theaters in the town nearby. I still remember the dress she wore and the smell of her favorite perfume. Lavender, she always smelled like fresh lavender." Lizzy awes at him and my heart compresses from his reminiscing.

We're quickly leaving the heart of town though, and as soon as I see the gated plot I say, "We're here dad." I look over at him and he's smiling. When we park, Lizzy clings to me as I'm sure she notices we're at a cemetery. My dad refuses to allow us to help him walk, relying on the same black cane my grandfather used to walk with.

We walk two steps behind him as he leads us to my mother's tombstone. When he reaches her, he says, "Hello my love, it's been too long, Angie." My heart constricts in my chest, and I think Lizzy senses it because she gives my arm a squeeze. It's nice to have her here with me. Normally when my dad and I come here, I wait in the car, almost always having nothing to say or the same 'I wish I knew you' speech. Looking down at Lizzy, I'm grateful she's here with me, and I briefly kiss the top of her head, quietly inhaling the sweet scent of mangos.

We listen to my dad say a few words when I hear him speak in a quieter tone saying, "I'm ready now Angie, I'm ready to follow your home." I don't know if Lizzy heard it, but I can't stand there anymore, so I grab her hand, signaling to go back to the truck.

Lizzy is suspicious of me.

After spending time with my father yesterday something made her say yes to moving in with me and as she remembers clearly, I told her I'd tell her if we we're on the same playing field.

Truthy, I think we always were. Every time she'd asked, I thought it was to make sure I wasn't falling off the deep end, to make sure it was just sex, but now after these past few months with her, I've realized she's fallen off the deep end with me.

I'm obsessed with her, I'm addicted to her, She's everything to me. I'm in love with her, but I don't just love her. I want her to be my wife. I want her to be the mother of my children, but we're not married yet, and I want to respect her wishes. Which brings me to where I am today sitting in the lobby of Cora Walkers Law firm.

After I dropped Lizzy off at her grandmother's house earlier today, I told her to pack her things, and I'd see her later. Since then, I've been texting her back slowly and accidentally on purpose, leaving her on read every time she asks me what I'm doing.

The front desk lady is typing away on her keyboard, and in the silence, the noise is intensified. The office isn't that large, but it's modernized with grey, black and white designs. I notice the only color here seems to be the fake mini bonsai tree sitting at the lobby desk.

"Mr. McCarter?" The front desk finally calls me, "She'll see you now." I nod in response and head to her office. Truthfully, I've never used her services before, I've only been here once or twice with Caleb as kids, he always hated it here.

When I enter, she's nowhere to be seen so I sit at her desk and wait. I ignore the little pictures she keeps of Caleb, because I know it's just for show. She only gives him attention when she wants something. A knot forms in my throat for some reason. I know what kind of person Cora is, after all she buries bodies both figuratively and literally.

She's a walking Devil. I have no real proof of this claim, but she always gives me shitty vibes and there's got to be a reason Caleb hates her so much. Nothing is ever unattainable for her, she'll do just about anything for her clients, or for *money*. Which makes her the perfect lawyer I guess, and exactly what I need.

Another five minutes pass and she walks in, "Daniel! What do I owe the pleasure?"

"I need to get married," I say, getting straight to the point. She laughs, "Well you need a Judge

THE SON OF A GHOST

for that not a Lawyer." I shake my head; I don't want to wait that long. I say, "No, right now, to Elizabeth Stone."

She laughs again, "Doesn't she need to be present for that?" I don't respond, growing impatient with her charades of morality. She clears her voice and sits up straighter, "You want me to forge a wedding certificate, pay off a judge to say he witnessed the union, and pay off a government employee to expedite the paperwork."

I nod saying, "You've done worse." We both know it. "I'll need Elizabeth's Signature along with a few documents from you."

I pull out an envelope from my back pocket with my ready documents saying, "You have Lizzy's paperwork from her divorce, so you are already her signature." I place the envelope down and she takes it saying, "I expect an upfront payment Daniel, but I'll give you a discount since this is our first transaction."

Yeah, and our last. "Just let me know when you're done." I say, seeing myself out, already thinking of how I'm going to surprise Lizzy with this. I know she'll be happy. I guess I could have gone the old-fashioned route and plan all the extremities of a proposal, then a wedding, but who knows how long that would have taken. I want her now. I want to get her pregnant right now. My father's distant voice plays in my mind telling me not to let her get away from me and that's exactly what I'm doing.

I want her for myself, forever and I know she wants me the same. From the moment she told me I'd be a great father, all I could do was picture her pregnant with my child, *our child*. She'll be happy, once I tell her.

As I get in my truck, my phone rings and I answer without checking the caller ID. "Hello," I say, putting on my seatbelt. "Danny! I swear to God, why aren't you answering my text?" Lizzy's voice sounds more relieved than harsh. I smile saying, "I'm sorry Lizzy, I was busy. All your stuff packed?"

She sighs through the phone, "It's been packed. For a while now Danny. Are you picking me up or am I meeting you there?"

"Meet me there," I reply, finally turning on the ignition, she says okay before hanging up. I toss my phone in the cab and speed home, hoping to beat her before she arrives.

I make it there with time to spare, rushing inside, excitement flows through me as I reach my bedroom and fish out my good old kink box and the brown paper bag with her gift that's been collecting dust under my bed since I made it for her. I stuff a black blindfold in my pocket, and I hear a text ping on my phone stating she's pulling up.

When she arrives, I meet her at the door, taking her bag. I say, "You made it in one piece." She smiles walking past me into the house, "I did. Are we going to talk about us now?" I close the door behind us, saying, "We are." I set her bag down and pull the blindfold out of my pocket, "But first I have a surprise."

Skeptical, she looks at me, saying, "Danny?"

I laugh, "Don't you trust me, Lizzy?" I gesture her to turn around so I can put it on her, and she replies, "I would if you weren't being so dang suspicious today." Quickly covering her eyes, I reply, "sorry about that. It's just been a busy day." Once the knot is secure, I ask, "Too tight?"

She moves her head to the left and right before responding, "No it's fine, I can't see a single thing though. Please don't guide me into the wall or something." I laugh again, taking her hand to lead her to the room. "No promises."

"Danny!" She whines but allows me to guide her. She's moving slow, but we make it into the room, and I guide her right to the edge of the bed before undressing her and saying, "I want you to crawl on the bed, and stay on all fours. Stop when your hands reach the pillows."

She takes a deep breath, then leans down onto the bed feeling around as she crawls up. I quickly shut the bedroom door and take my shirt off in the process. "Now what?" Lizzy asks from the bed. I move to grab the brown bag, admiring her nakedness on my bed as I reply, "You remember that gift I said I made you for your divorce?" She replies quickly, "Yes."

"Well now I get to show it to you," First, I pull out the custom-made toy, and instead of showing her, I lightly rub it against her pussy. Her body jolts from the sudden contact before she replies, "Is that…Is that a dildo, Danny?"

Continuing to rub it against her I reply, "Not just any dildo baby, it's my cock, a perfect replica, molded just for you." I rub the tip at her entrance where my piercing would be. She laughs a little, saying, "You made me a replica of your cock. My god, Danny, why on earth would you do that?" I can't help but smile, though she can't see me, "So I can stuff you all at once. Just don't ask me how difficult it was to stay hard long enough for the mold to set."

She laughs at this, and I finally drop the toy to kneel behind her. "But first…" I trail off, lowering my head to her pussy. Determined to eat her from the back, I continue, "Be a doll and stay still for me baby. There are no restraints to keep you in place this time."

"Okay," she says breathlessly, and I wrap my arms around her waist, not waiting another moment before digging in. She squeals when my tongue meets her lips, and I can't stop the groan that leaves my throat when the taste of her floods my mouth. Being this close to her skin, I can smell her signature scent of mangos and my cock throbs.

The sound of her moans fills the room as my tongue explores her. I swear she can feed me just like this for the rest of my life. Dinner, dessert, appetizer, I don't care, as long as I can keep her sweetness on my tongue. She moans my name, and I adjust to focus on her clit. She moans louder, "That feels so good!" Her voice sends a volt of blood rushing straight to my cock, okay maybe I can feast and *fuck* her for the rest of my life. I double my efforts to bring an orgasm rushing through her, before I rise, desperate to be inside of her.

She whines a little but doesn't say anything as she listens to the sound of me unboxing the other part to her toy, "What is that?"

"The part that makes the toy work," I reply quickly setting up the fuck machine behind her. Grabbing some lube, I slide the replica onto the machine and angle it at her entrance. She waits patiently, as I drizzle some on the toy and her asshole.

After, I find the small remote and turn it on. She gaps when it immediately starts fucking her and my dick throbs with excitement. I could have made a second one to fill her throat, but I love hearing her moan too much. I move, settling myself above the machine and at her back entrance. I stroke myself in hand before beginning to push inside her. Fuck, she so tight here. She cries out, her body tensing, even with the lube it's a struggle, but she sits there and takes it, "Look at you Lizzy doll, being such a good girl and letting me stuff you with my cocks." I intentionally use the plural, and she whines in response.

I pull out a little, and push back in, cursing under my breath as to how good she feels around me. I sink further in saying, "That's it baby, let me in that sweet ass of yours." Her cries are mixing with her moans, and soon I'm able to slide in and out with ease and dammit it feels so good, "That's it. Look at you taking both my cocks. Do you like being stuffed?"

"Yes! Danny oh god!" She moans in response and my dick pulses inside her.

Heaven. That's what she feels like, "That's it baby, let me hear those pretty sounds of yours." I slow my stroke, not wanting to come before she does, "Touch yourself Lizzy, I want to feel you come." She moves slowly, slipping her left hand down to her clit.

"You want to know how I feel about you Lizzy, want to know exactly where we stand?" I question through gritted teeth, trying to prolong my release.

"Yes," She replies quickly, lost in the pleasure.

"Come for me and I'll tell you." I say and within a few more minutes, she does. Crying out, as the toy and I still pump inside her.

On the brink of coming, I tell her what she needs to hear, "You own my soul, Lizzy. There is no playing field. We're not just friends with benefits, this pussy is mine. You are mine. We're going to get married and you're going to be my little wife." *and bare my children.* I keep that part to myself unable to hold back, I come inside of her ass, and she squeals from the feeling.

14. She Liked Her Surprise & Now We're Going Thrifting

DANIEL

After forcing a few more orgasms out of her, Lizzy lays sleeping next to me. I make a mental note of no more anal until I get her pregnant and wonder how I'm going to tell her we're already married so she lets me.

Lizzy's phone rings from the hall, and I'm sure it's still in her bag. I try to move and not wake her but as soon as I do, she stirs. "Is that my phone?" she asks sleepily. I nod as she blinks her eyes a few times, "I'll go get it. Go ahead and rest."

I pull on a pair of gym shorts before leaving her in the room, as I walk down the hall, excitement bubbles in my stomach as I think about how we'll spend our days here. Will she want to redecorate? Will we raise our kids here?

I find her phone in the side pocket of her duffle bag, and I see Hazel's caller ID. I answer it, walking back to the bedroom, "Hi Hazel."

"Daniel?" she questions on the other line. "Yup, that's me. What's up?" I ask, entering the bedroom to see Lizzy still in bed. "Even better, August and I wanted to do some last-minute shopping and wanted Liz to tag along. I take it she's with you right now so you can come too if you want." Lizzy stirs but her eyes stay closed as I sit beside her in bed, "Sounds like a plan, Lizzy's napping though. I'll ask her when she wakes." Lizzy nuzzles up beside me as Hazel responds, "Okay, just let me know. I want to leave within the hour." We hang up the phone and I lean down, smelling Lizzy's hair. This wakes her.

"What are you doing, Danny." Her voice is sheepish and low as she wakes. "Getting my daily dose of you," I say, smiling down at her. Her eyes blink a few times as she sits up, "So, just to clarify, we're dating now, right? I'm yours and you're mine?"

I laugh, "I thought declaring you owner of my soul meant as much yeah." Fully awake now, she smacks my arm playfully, "Oh whatever Danny, I'm just being sure." I laugh more, finally telling her about the phone call. "Of course I want to go shopping, we're stepping into the colder months soon, and I only have summer clothes." She says excitedly, reaching for her phone to call Hazel Back. I guess we're going then.

"The baby doesn't need a snowboarding outfit, August," Hazel shakes her head at the newborn size black puffy snowsuit August is holding up. They're standing in the aisle across from us, while Lizzy and I are watching in amusement. August replies, "Why not, it's perfect for winter." We're currently in a thrift store in the heart of town, looking at baby clothes as if August and Hazel didn't get a shit ton from their baby shower. There's only a handful of other people here, so they aren't really making a scene.

Hazel gives Lizzy a knowing look before rolling her eyes at August, "Yes, but it's newborn size and when winter comes, Everson will probably be too big to fit it."

August argues back, "His name is June, and I'll just get a bigger size."

Hazel says, "No, put it back and we haven't agreed on his name yet." Lizzy and I finally burst out laughing when August makes a face of mischief before he glares at us. "See what I mean," Lizzy tells me as she picks up a random baby boy outfit before putting it down and picking up another. "I do," I reply, watching the faces she makes when she sees one she likes. "This one or That?" Hazel calls her from across the rack. One's a brown and white romper; the other is a purple and orange pants set. Lizzy replies, "I like the brown one."

Hazel agrees and Lizzy begins to walk to a different section and of course I follow her. She's looking at a long sleeve winter dress when she asks, "Are we going to act like that over baby clothes?" I smile because she's thinking about having babies with me, "I think most couples do, unfortunately." She shakes her head but smiles as she pulls out a grey winter dress from the rack, "Why are all the winter dress colorless? I want a pink one, or yellow. These are all brown, tan, or black."

Unsatisfied, she begins placing them back on the rack, but I stop her, "How about you go try them on. I bet you'll still look delicious in them either way." She debates a moment before she agrees, and I follow her to the back of the store where some dressing rooms are.

She picks one, and I stand in front of the curtain like door. I hear her undressing when Hazel passes by me with a few dresses of her own, walking into the one right next to her. August is following right behind her and joins me saying, "Well this is fun."

"I can think of a few things that are much more fun," I reply, and he laughs. We stand there for a few minutes listening to them to change when he says, "So you're serious about her, huh Daniel? I've never seen you this sprung out over any girl, ever." I nod, "I'm not sprung out, I'm obsessed. There's a difference." He shakes his head in amusement before continuing, "So you plan on marrying her and having kids? Growing old together, the whole nine yards?"

This time I lower my voice when I respond, "We're already married, she just doesn't know it yet." Well almost, I'm still waiting for the text from Cora.

"What do you mean she doesn't know?"

"I mean legally-ish, she's mine and I may or may not being trying to get her pregnant already." I say and he almost laughs, almost. Until he sees the expression on my face. He replies, "Oh Daniel, you are so far gone. Straight off a cliff and into the deep. Do me a favor don't get arrested for falling in love with this girl."

Love. Is that what this is? No, I don't think love is the right word, it's too mundane, too simply put. Before I can respond though, Lizzy opens the curtain, but doesn't step out of the dressing room. The brown sweater dress looks cute on her, but she's got her arms crossed with her bottom lip puckered out, saying, "This is hideous."

She's pouting and I can't help but laugh, "You look adorable." I begin walking into the room, not caring if someone sees us. "I don't want to look adorable, I want to look sexy, and this doesn't make me feel sexy." She turns around to face herself in the mirror and I close the curtain behind us.

"I think you look sexy, but you know what I'd think look even sexier?" I say walking up behind her, and she watches me in the mirror as my hands move around her waist and begin to cup the lower side of her belly. I turn her slightly in the mirror, before whispering in her ear, "I think you would look a thousand times sexier, if there was a baby growing in here."

Her brain takes a moment to process my words before she smacks her lips and pushes my hands away, "Don't play with me like that, that's not funny." Turning her around to face me I say, "Who's says I'm laughing?" She looks up into my eyes saying, "Danny you can't be serious, we've barely made it official *today*. I don't want to joke about a serious matter."

How do I make this woman see that I'm not joking? I push her against the wall, running my fingers along her curves and press my body into hers as I move to whisper in her ear, "Tell me Lizzy, if I tied you to my bed and fucked you full of my cum, would you stop me?" Her voice catches in her throat as she lets out a broken whimper. I continue moving my fingers under her dress, "If I kept you there, filling you up like it's my god damn calling. Tell me you don't want that?" I ask, feeling the heat of her skin as I rub my hand across her belly.

"I uh, I'd," She begins trying to find her words. We're interrupted though, by an unfamiliar voice, "Excuse me miss? It's only one person per dressing room; I'm going to have to ask you to step out and wait for the other person to finish."

I kiss her head before taking a step back, nodding at her to respond. She looks baffled while saying, "Okay, sorry! I'll be out in a second."

After we hear the associate leave, I leave saying, "Try on the next dress, I'll be outside."

My alarm wakes me up at 10:30a.m., As I sit up, I realize my bed is empty and a panic develops in my chest. Just as I'm throwing the blankets off of me, Lizzy comes out of the bathroom, freshly showered, in a mismatched blue bra and black panties.

"Morning," She smiles at me, and I have to take a deep breath to calm my heart rate. Normally, I'm awake before she is. "You're up early," I say, moving to get out of bed to give her a kiss. "Well, I wanted to make sure I had enough time to get ready for church." She kisses me back when I reach her before turning to grab her lotion.

"Can't we stay home today?" I ask. Cara messaged me late last night, that everything is finalized, Lizzy's all mine, and that the marriage certificate will be sent. I was thinking of taking her out to surprise her.

"No, we have to go. The church is blessing Justin's travels today and I'd like to be there for his support."

"Okay. I guess I'll go get ready then."

It doesn't take me long to find a suit to wear, and soon enough we're heading out the door. We make it to the church just before the service begins and even though Lizzy's family is sitting towards the front of the church, she agrees to sit in the back with me, where my dad and I always sit.

Pastor Forkhill begins service with a prayer before he addresses the church, "Good morning brothers and sisters. I recently spoke with a saddened soul, he asked; how do we keep our faith in God, when it feels like God has lost his faith in us?"

He begins to dive into why our faith shouldn't waiver, but I keep getting distracted by the warmth of Lizzy's body touching mine. She's sitting on my left, and our thighs are touching but I want to feel more of her. So, I wrap my arm around her and pull her close into me. She smiles but doesn't say anything. Much better.

The Pastor's normal service takes a turn after thirty minutes when he asks Justin to come to the front. Pastor John places his right hand on his shoulder, "Justin, you've been a member of the church for a long time and now you seek a different journey. I have spoken with God about the new path you take, and he wishes you well."

I glance down to see Lizzy's lip quiver, and I hold her a little tighter. Justin nods his head as the pastor continues, "Let us pray over Justin's new path in life and wish him safe travels. If everyone could bow their heads with me."

As he begins praying, I feel Lizzy's right-hand reach for my left and we listen to Pastor Forkhill speak, "Heavenly father, we come to you today to ask that you watch over Justin and guide him in his new walk in life. Protect him from the things that could lead him astray and bless him with your unwavering love. In Jesus' name we pray, amen." The church erupts in amens and Pastor Forkhill pulls Justin in for a hug.

When the service is over, we linger with the crowd, Justin isn't leaving today but the church sure is acting like it. Multiple people crowd him, giving him hugs and well wishes. I barge through them though, so Lizzy can say hi to her cousin. "Justin!" She yells as soon as we reach him. He smiles down at her before pulling her into a hug. We greet each other before I glance over at Cathy to see her standing nearby with tears in her eyes.

"Can I be honest?" Lizzy says when they pull away from each other. He replies, "Brutally honest or just honest?" She laughs and reaches for my hand, "Just honest."

"Then yes," Justin says. As he replies, another church member, I think her name is Anna, butts in to greet him. "You've grown into such a handsome young man Justin; we're going to miss you," she says. Anna doesn't even apologize for interrupting, but Justin responds with no problem, "Thank you Anna. I appreciate it. I'm sorry again for your loss."

Lizzy and I stand nearby as she smiles at him before pulling him into another hug, "Thank you, Kim would have been happy to see you off." The mention of Kim makes me a little uneasy, but I say nothing as we wait for her to pass. Kim disappeared before Lizzy arrived so, of course, she's unaffected.

As Anna walks away, Lizzy resumes speaking, "I was going to say, I hate that you're leaving but I am happy you're following your dreams." He laughs, "Well I think it's time. Mamma Cathy will be fine now that she has you and Suzie in town." Lizzy agrees as August and Hazel approach us. "We'll miss you, Justin!" Hazel pulls him into a hug, well as much as a hug her belly will allow. "I'll miss you too Hazel," he replies.

She then greets both Lizzy and I. "It was a pleasure to go to know you Justin," August says as he pulls Hazel back towards him. Hazel wipes her eyes saying, "Dammit I promised myself I wouldn't cry today!"

Lizzy chimes in, "I'm trying not to get emotional either. The real goodbyes start tomorrow."

Justin responds softly, "Well at least I know you care." August gives him a weird look that neither Hazel nor Lizzy notices. "You're going to come to the fundraiser today, right?" Hazel asks him, still wiping her eyes. "Of course we will," Justin says excitedly, and Lizzy agrees.

We talk a little more before we decided to head home to change and meet up at the fundraiser. Apparently, it's sponsored by Mwenzi's Wine, the same wine company that the church uses for Communion.

When Lizzy and I arrive, the setup is already done, and people are moving happily about. There's a section for a pie contest and an area for face painting. The sponsor's banner is near the popcorn machine and there's even a ticket raffle for a wine gift basket.

People from all over town are here, not just church members, but people I've seen at the shop before, older faces I recognize from high school. Even Maxxie's here in his old grease-stained work shirt. My dad would have loved to see the whole town together. I wonder, did everyone close early just to be here?

"There you guys are!" Hazel calls out to us, and we move to approach her. Before she can say anything, I see August and Caleb standing nearby the drinks, so I dismiss myself and head towards them. "There's our favorite lover boy!" Caleb teases at my approach and August grins.

I greet them with handshakes before replying, "Yeah, yeah fuck off." August hands me a cold beer as he says, "Not just any Loverboy, he's an *obsessed* Loverboy. Has he told you yet, Caleb. He's already married to Lizzy, *and* she doesn't know." I quickly open the beer taking a sip as Caleb teases, "Look at little D, taking a trip to the dark side. Be careful now, there's no sunshine or rainbows here." They both laugh and I sip my beer shaking my head, "I don't need sunshine or rainbows as long as I have her."

"Is Liz made of magic? I need some of that because the way she has you knotted up like a bull, makes me think she's got fairy dust between her legs or some shit," Caleb jokes and I feel a flash of heat run down my spine. August replies first, "He's going to fuck you up Caleb, better stop talking about his girl."

"Caleb, bestie, I love you, but I will fucking kill you if you touch Lizzy," I say with a straight face, but Caleb only laughs. August joins him and soon we're laughing.

I continue, "You think I'm crazy now, but watch when you find someone you can't see your life without. You'll probably be worse than me."

"Probably, but I'm not looking so who knows." he agrees. After our shits and giggles, we turn to find Hazel and Lizzy getting their faces painted together. Lizzy's got an orange flower on her face and Hazel's got a small black bird. Lizzy laughs at something she says before her eyes find mine. *Fuck.* That's my wife. That's my fucking wife.

She smiles and waves at me before her attention turns back to Hazel. I almost regret not marrying her properly just to see her in a wedding dress and telling the whole town that she belongs to me. *Almost.*

"So why is Mwenzi sponsoring this event again," The sound of Caleb's voice recaptures my attention. August replies, "Because they used to be close friends with my dad and owes him a favor." August replies, killing the rest of his beer.

Caleb does the same saying, "Not really an explanation but okay pastor boy, or should we call you Pastor Daddy now." Both Caleb and I crack up at this. August just smiles and says, "There's only two people I'm okay will calling me that and it's not you fuckers."

15. Revelations & Goodbyes

ELIZABETH

I look over at Daniel who's standing with August and Caleb. He's already staring at me, so I smile and wave before Hazel says, "Seriously though, the more I hear it, the more I like the name June. I still like Everson more, so maybe we can come to an agreement." she rubs her belly as she speaks.

She's trying not to move so much as the artist finishes up her face painting, mine is already done. "I'm sure you guys will agree on something," I reply, checking out the flower on my face through a mini mirror.

"I hope so," she agrees before continuing, "So you and Daniel, you guys are serious huh?" I haven't updated her yet about us moving in together, but I suppose it's obvious. "Yeah, we are now," I begin as the artist dismisses us. Hazel takes a moment to stand, shooing my offered hand away.

She sighs in relief when she's completely upright saying, "God this boy makes me feel so huge sometimes." She takes a deep breath before continuing, "anyway are you happy with him?" We glance back at the guys who seem to be laughing their heads off about something.

I smile, "I am. Do you think we're rushing into it? I know we've only known each other for a few months." She shakes her, "Nonsense, Liz. I had to wait eight years for mine, so if yours wants you only after a few months, I say go for it. I just want to make sure you're happy with him."

THE SON OF A GHOST

I smile again, "I am so happy with him Hazel. He's been so supportive through my divorce, not judging me for my rowdy family. He cares about me and has such a good heart it makes mine overflow. I've seen him at work, he goes the extra mile for others and God, I know he's going to make such a great dad one day."

I pause, reflecting on all the time Daniel and I've spent together. I smile before saying, "I love him Hazel, I love him so much."

She grins at me saying, "Well in that case, I wish you all the world's happiness, and who knows maybe you'll get married and pop out a kid or two so our kids can be besties." She rubs her belly again, not knowing just how much I'd love another chance to be a parent.

Two girls I loosely recognize from the church walk up to us saying, "Hazel! It's so good to see you!" I don't remember their names, but they seem to know Hazel enough. They chat about the event, and I stand there trying not to be awkward. After a moment they thank Hazel before disappearing.

"Well, it seems like you're pretty popular with the church," I say as we continue walking to no particular destination. She laughs, "I wouldn't frame it as popularity, but we did help a lot at the food drives. That's where most of them know me from and that I'm married to the Pastor's son."

We laugh and I spot a pie eating contest nearby, "Oh my God! We should join in!"

The fundraiser event was surprisingly fun. Hazel and I lost the pie competition but really, I just enjoyed eating the pie. We even got to take a few bottles of Mwenzi Wine home.

Now though, it's twelve o'clock noon, and we're waiting with Justin at the airport. Daniel had to be at the shop, Carson is overseeing the new staff at the salon, and our parents went home, so it's just me, Suzie, Clay, and Mamma Cathy saying goodbye. "Don't tell me you're going to move to Va'More? That place is littered with tourists and pick pocketers," Suzie asks as we stand in a circle waiting for his flight to be called.

THE SON OF A GHOST

"Well, it's just for now. I haven't decided if it'll be a permanent thing yet," he replies, moving his large duffle bag from one shoulder to the other. For some reason the action makes my heart hurt. Everything he owns is packed up in the gym bag, he's really moving on from little ol' Springville.

"You promise to call once a week?" I say, my voice is full of emotions I'm trying to hide. He laughs, "I won't miss a single phone call." I glance at Mamma Cathy, the smile on her face is an emotional one.

Clay tries to lighten the mood saying, "You guys, stop being so dramatic, he's not moving across the globe." We laugh, and she continues, "But seriously we'll miss you cousin. If you blow up and become a famous DJ, don't forget about us."

He shakes his head but says, "I won't." Mamma Cathy finally speaks, saying, "I am so proud of you Justin. Your mother, she would have been proud, so proud of you baby." Before he can reply she pulls him into an embrace. My eyes begin to swell and dammit, the tears.

We hear his flight number, and we say goodbye all over again, until he begins putting space between us saying, "I love you guys, but I can't miss my flight." I try to laugh away the heartache I feel. I know this isn't a bad thing. He's got his own life to live; he deserves a chance at happiness just like the rest of us. It's bittersweet.

My sisters move closer to me, each reaching to hold one of my hands as we watch as he walks away. We don't turn until he leaves our sight. God, if you can still hear me, please watch over him. Mamma Cathy takes a deep breath before turning to us and saying, "He'll be okay. Come on, now that I got the keys to the old flower shop. I think it's about time we go see what we're working with and get it cleaned up." Suzie, Clay, and I agree as we follow her out of the airport.

We ride in comfortable silence in my little Betsy; Mamma Cathy sits in the passenger seat while Suzie and Clay sit in the back. I have the radio playing on low and it's still daylight out but you can feel the smallest breeze, a hint of the season soon to change.

"So, are you going to re-open the flower shop or turn it into something else?" I ask Mamma Cathy as we drive through town.

"I want to reopen it as is, but first I need to see the condition it's in," she replies. I know likes to keep busy, but I wonder if she really wants to start up another business. The town already loves her; she's financially taken care of. Why doesn't she just want to spend the rest of her life in peace. "Mamma Cathy," I begin slowly.

The caution in my voice has Suzie and Clay peaking up to listen. "Why don't we just go home and not open the shop. Suzie and I both live in town now. We can spend more time together baking and learning all of your recipes," I say keeping my tone light, in hopes she doesn't see it as an accusation.

Mamma Cathy smacks her lips saying, "Nonsense child. We can still bake *and* open the shop." She isn't snapping at me, so I press on, "But *why* Mamma Cathy? Why do you want to open this flower shop? Besides not resting and wanting to stay busy?"

She doesn't respond for a moment before simply saying, "Because God told me to, Elizabeth. I've always felt a pull to that old flower shop; you and your sister just gave me the excuse to finally do something about it." She uses my government name and the whole car is silent. Our full names are only used if we were getting in trouble, but there's no conviction in her voice.

Unsure, Suzie tries to change the subject by saying, "Liz, are we almost there? I really have to pee."

"Yeah, we're almost there," I say letting it go because what do you say to refute God.

When we finally arrive, the inside looks dark and spooky from the window. I have a feeling this place has been closed for a long time. As Mamma Cathy finally takes out the key my phone pings with a text from Danny.

My love: I miss you :(
Me: I miss you too
My love: I have a surprise for you
Me: More surprises?
My love: It's the best surprise!

As I'm texting, Mamma Cathy, Suzie, and Clay have already gone inside. I follow suit, just as Clay finds the lights. Half of them are broken but the space lights up. It's a small shop; dust and cobwebs cover every inch of the place. There's a bunch of fixtures covered in sheets and there are empty shelves on the walls. "Um, are you sure about this?" Suzie asks, while keeping close to Clay.

"Yes. Now Clay, can you go get the cleaning supplies out of the trunk. Come on girls, let's start with the sheets." I flex my fingers before reaching to pull off one next to me and the window, which reveals a small table with two chairs.

"You don't have to tell me twice," Clay says heading towards the door, she passes by me to grab my keys on the way out. "Can I wait for the gloves?" Suzie asks, but the look Mamma Cathy gives her is definitely a no.

We start cleaning what we can, Suzie wipes down the storefront windows, and Clay takes some old pottery pieces to the trash. We wipe down the counters, the tables, even clean the walls and before we know it, the shop no longer looks spooky. "Liz, take those sheets to the back dumpster please.

We've done all we can today." Mamma Cathy asks, and I nod in response. I grab the pile of dirty sheets and head out the back door.

The back door creaks as I walk through it, and the dumpster sits in a small alleyway. The sun is still out so it doesn't look scary as I toss the old sheets in the bin.

Back inside, Clay's gathered the supplies, while Mamma Cathy and Suzie are waiting by the door. As I pass through the clean white room, I ask, "Are you going to paint the walls or leave them as is?"

When I reach her, she responds, "I want to leave the walls how they are, but I want to hang a few paintings." She turns off the light and locks the door behind us. "Okay, just let me know when, I'm happy to help!" Though I still don't understand her reasoning, I can already see the place full of plants and her herbal jars, Greenery hanging from the ceiling and covering the walls. The new project is kind of exciting.

Afterwards, I take everyone home.

At sunset, I find myself pulling into Danny's driveway, *our* driveway. Gosh I have to get use to that. He's waiting in front of the door with that

THE SON OF A GHOST

horribly boyish grin of his. As I get out of the car and approach him, I'm hit with an overwhelming feeling of warmth and contentment.

"Hi," I say as the feeling washes over me. "Hi Lizzy. Ready for your surprise?" He smiles and starts to lead me to his truck. I protest, saying, "Wait, I have to pee."

He drops my hand saying, "Okay, hurry though, I'll wait in the truck." I nod in response heading into the house and straight to the hallway bathroom.

I don't take long, finding my way around easily, it's almost unbelievable how much my life has changed since moving here. Sometimes I'm still worried we're moving too fast, but Danny seems to love me as much as I love him. He hasn't said it yet, but I know it's there between us. Danny is my person.

"Lizzy!" I hear his voice call me from the front door. So impatient. "Coming!" I yell, finishing up and headed back to the door. He waits in the threshold, as I hear his car idling in the background. "I was only in there for like a minute," I say approaching him. He responds dramatically, "I know I could have died or something. That's far too much time away from me Lizzy, next time you should just take me with you." He looks down at me and I pat his cheek, "Next time I'll bring you to the bathroom with me, but be warned, if I have to crap, you might die anyway."

He makes a face saying, "Yeah on second thought, maybe I'll just guard the door." This makes me laugh, "I thought so." He smiles leaning down to kiss me and butterflies erupt in my stomach. As he pulls away, he finds my hand and leads us out the door saying, "Okay now we can go."

I have no idea where we're going. Though I keep guessing, considering I've become familiar with a few places, I thought for sure he was taking me to the café or even somewhere in the next town over. Imagine my surprise when his car comes to a slow halt at the town line. "Um, are we here?" I ask, as I see the vaguely familiar abandoned church come into view.

He nods as he cuts the engine, "Well I wanted to take you somewhere I thought was meaningful." I nod, "Okay?" waiting for him to continue.

"This is where we first met, Lizzy," He states unbuckling his seatbelt to turn towards me. My face softens at the realization as I say, "When Betsy broke down." He nods and memories of that night flash in my mind. The wounds are still there but they don't hurt as much. The memories feel so distant now.

He begins to pull something out of his pocket, "It's not the official thing, that takes a few weeks to come in the mail, but I wanted to show you anyway." My heartrate picks up, is he going to propose? A mix of excitement and nervousness bloom inside me, but as he pulls out a folded piece of paper, I try to calm my nerves.

"What is it?" I ask, confused as he hands it to me. He doesn't answer as he watches me unfold it. "Certification of Marriage?" I say out loud, reading my name, his and a signature that's definitely mine, but I don't remember signing. "Danny what is this?" I hold up the paper, my confusion turning into frustration. He takes it back from me saying, "It's our marriage certificate, Lizzy; we're married. I wanted to surprise you with it."

"You're joking." I say immediately. I mean of course I'd love to marry him, eventually. He shakes his head as a response. "How is that legal? This has to be a joke, Danny. We haven't gone in front of a judge, there hasn't been a wedding, you haven't even asked for my father's blessing. That can't be real." I say, as the panic rises inside me.

Danny scoots across the cab to still me, "Lizzy, calm down baby, everything's okay. I can still ask him, and if you still want a wedding, we can have that too. I just didn't want to spend any more time untied to you. Don't you see, Lizzy Doll? I want to be yours forever and I want a family with you; I want everything with you baby."

His words do nothing to calm me. I yell, "That's not the point Daniel! You didn't even ask me! That's not right, why would you do that? This is too much!" He is silent as he slowly removes his hands from my arms. I see the confusion written on his face, but can't he see the hurt in mine?

His voice is low as he speaks, "I thought you'd be happy, Lizzy." Happy? "I…" I begin but stop myself because isn't this what I wanted? A man to love me, a family of my own. But we've only been together for so long, he could still change up on me and I'd be back in the same situation I was running from.

"I am happy with you, Danny," I take a deep breath and continue, "I just, I need a moment. I need space to think about this. You've gone behind my back, forged a marriage certificate, which I'm pretty sure is a crime and I don't even want to know how you made that happen. Just take me to my grandmother's house, please?"

He takes a moment to respond before nodding and starting his truck. I feel like I'm overreacting, but if the roles were reversed, he'd be upset too. The entire ride back into town is silent. We just started dating, we're still learning about each other. I rushed into my last marriage and ended up divorced. I don't want that to happen again.

When he pulls in front of my grandmother's house, I almost don't want to go inside. I feel like we haven't been away from each other since we made it official, but I open the door saying, "I'm upset with you, but I still care. I'll call you tomorrow." Before I move to leave, he says, "I'm sorry Lizzy, I didn't think you'd be this upset, I thought you wanted the same things I did."

His words hurt. That's not fair; he knows I want a family, marriage, a happy home, but not like this. So, I don't respond as I get out of the car, and I don't look back as I hear his truck idle as I make my way to the door. Thankfully, my grandmother answers. I still don't look back as I walk in, and she closes the door behind me.

"Are you okay baby?" she asks as I follow her to the kitchen. I nod, "Yeah, I'm okay." Truthfully, I am fine, I'm not sad, I just feel…betrayed? "Then what's wrong baby, I thought you moved in with Daniel?" She walks to the counter setting up fresh herbs to dry out, while I take a seat at the table. "I'm scared," I finally say.

"Oh honey, relationships are nothing to be scared of. You can't go running every time something bad happens."

"But what if this is a mistake, Mamma Cathy? I love him, I think I've been in love with him far longer than I realized, and I'm terrified. He went behind my back and if I dismiss it now, I feel like I'm setting myself up to be used or lied to again."

She moves to the sink as she replies, "Has he hurt you?"

"No."

"Do you think he'll ever hurt you?"

I shake my head, "No."

"Then honey, you can't let fear stop you from being in love," she says, grabbing a wet jar from the sink and begins drying it. "If what he's done isn't hurting you and you love him, then go back to him. Let him know how you feel and find a solution. You think I ran every time your grandfather hurt my feelings. Honey, sometimes people do things that may be stupid to you but make sense to them. Talk to him."

16. A Stubborn Woman, Death, & Danny

ELIZABETH

It's been a few days since Danny told me we were "married". I haven't intentionally been ignoring him, it's just, okay, I have. I've come to terms with it, it's not like that wasn't the goal anyway. I do love him, so I just need to talk to him and let him know that he can't do things like that, and I do still want a proper wedding.

The thing is though, every time I tell myself I'm going to call and talk to him, I end up not doing so. Mamma Cathy and I are in the flower shop today cleaning up some more. Really, we're just wiping down surfaces, considering we've already cleaned, deep cleaned, and blessed the room.

The first few sets of vases and plants should be arriving today too, so that's exciting. "Has Clay let you know she made it home yet?" Mamma Cathy calls from behind the counter. I stop wiping the windows to check my phone. Clay hasn't sent anything but my phone rings with a call from Justin, which I answer and put on speaker phone, "Justin!" Mamma Cathy's head perks up at the mention of his name.

"Hey Liz, I'm just checking in with you guys!" His voice sounds louder in the semi empty space. "It's good to hear from you! How are you settling in?" A smile erupts on Mamma Cathy's face as she stops what she's doing to come closer to the phone.

"I'm doing good, I made a few friends I'm going to be roommates with someone until I save up a little more for this studio I want, but things are good. How's the shop coming along?"

Mamma Cathy replies, "Hey baby, the shop is doing fine, it's slowly coming together. You be careful rooming with people, just because they're smiling in your face doesn't mean they've got your back."

"I know Moms, I'm being careful." He replies with a laugh. I ask, "Have you gotten any gigs yet?" Mamma Cathy beckons me over to the small table for us to sit. "Yeah, actually I have one later tonight, it's a small club, and it's still new so I'll see how the vibe is."

"That's good to hear Justin, I'm glad you're adjusting well," I reply sitting down.

"Yeah, so when will the shop open? Have you picked a name for it yet?" He asks.

"Oh, we still have a few weeks, and some paperwork we're waiting on before we can officially open and I'm not giving it a name. God's told me to leave it as it is," She says and I frown at her response. God sure is guiding her closely these days. Justin also doesn't comment on her statement and wishes us well saying he'll call next week.

When we get off the phone, we get back to cleaning and I spill some dirty water on my top, "Dang it!" Mamma Cathy makes a face at me and says, "That's your sign to either call Daniel and go back home, or move back in with me and get some new clothes. You've been in that outfit for two days now."

I try wiping my shirt but of course the water seeps in, "Yes ma'am." I mentally roll my eyes because getting my clothes dirty can't possibly correlate with calling Danny. Suddenly, I hear a truck pull up out front and I say, "The pots are here!"

A man with the name tag Mike, lets me sign off the papers and even helps us unload boxes before he leaves. We begin opening the boxes and deciding where to place some when Mamma Cathy cries out in pain, "Oh lord my back!"

She pauses hunched over one of the boxes and panic rises in me, "Mamma Cathy?" I hurry over to her as she's trying to slowly stand up straight with her right hand on her hip. I notice she is struggling though as she moans in pain. "What's wrong?" I ask as I reach her, grabbing her arm and shoulder.

"It's my back baby; it's locking up again. I just need to sit down for a moment."

"Again?" I repeat but still help her move to sit. How long has she been dealing with this? "Do me a favor and rub small circles on my back until I can sit straight," She asks, and I move to do so immediately. Who was doing this for her before? Does Justin know?

After ten minutes of massaging her back her muscles relax and she's able to sit straight. "How long has that been happening?" I finally ask. She takes a deep breath, saying, "It doesn't happen often." I shake my head because that doesn't really answer the question. I ask, "Is opening this store going to be a problem for you Mamma Cathy?"

"No, I'll be fine baby, it's nothing," She tries to dismiss my concern. "Mamma Cathy, if I can't be here when that happens, what then? Justin is gone, Suzie's pregnant and can't help in the shop. I don't think this is a good idea, not for your body anyway."

"Girl hush, I will be fine."

Frustrated, I walk away and decide to take a breather outside. Her body clearly can't handle the hard work anymore and she still refuses to retire. I decide to text Justin about it and he replies quickly, telling me it happens occasionally only when she works her body too hard. Good Lord. I groan in frustration. What's going to make this woman cave?

After calming down I go back inside to find her placing some of the smaller pots on the shelf for display. I finish helping her for the day, making sure to keep an extra watch on her. When she sends me out of the shop door, telling me she'll close up, I guess I have no choice but to talk with Danny. I glance across the street at Maxxie's Diner and an apple pie seems like the perfect motivation.

So, I check my phone, honestly surprised he hasn't tried blowing it up with calls or texts and send him a quick message, letting him know I want to talk later. Then I head across the street. The Diner is in the heart of town so it's a little busy here, but the pedestrians and motor vehicles are cordial.

When I make it to the front door, I can see someone just about to walk out, so I open the door for them. "Thank you–*oh*! Liz, it's good to see you!" Cora, my lawyer, walks out in her custom fit purple and white blazer with a white bag of food in her hand. "Hi, Cora. It's nice seeing you too. I rarely see you around town, how are you doing?"

"Yeah, I prefer to stick to the walls of the firm, but my assistant took off today so had to grab lunch myself," she shakes the bag and smiles before someone walks by and says excuse me. We move from the doorway further outside when she asks, "How have you been settling in town? I've heard a lot of town buzz about your family this month?"

Town buzz? Does she mean gossip? "Well, I hope you've heard nothing but positive things," I laugh not trying to let her words rub me the wrong way as I'm sure she doesn't mean anything behind. "I've been settling in just fine. Though, I'll admit so much has changed in such a short time."

"I forgot who told me, but your oldest sister took over your grandmother's hair salon right? Your Grandmother chose to reopen that old flower shop, oh that poor thing? How is she handling all of these changes?"

"She's doing well," I say not showing my concern, though if I had it my way Mamma Cathy would be sitting in the living room, in a rocking chair doing safe granny hobbies like knitting. "Well, that's good, you know they've had that shop since I was a little girl. It's a little sad she's letting it go so easily."

Her comment surprises me a little, she has no idea how difficult she's been. I reply, "It's still in the family though, so it's not too bad."

"I suppose that's not bad at all. Oh! You and Daniel are clearly a thing now. How's that going?" I smile at the mention of Danny's name, saying, "It's been intense, to say the least."

"I'm sure it has. Well, I've got to get going. It was nice running into you," She dismisses herself with a smile and I wave goodbye after her. Continuing my original task, I stroll inside the diner, determined to have a nice hot apple pie before I meet Danny.

After eating not one but two apple pies, I hurry back to Mamma Cathy's house to make sure she

THE SON OF A GHOST

made it home safe. Then, *then* I'll meet with Daniel. As I walk through the door, I hear her voice coming from the kitchen, "Elizabeth?"

"Yep, it's me," I reply, closing the door behind me, walking to join her in the kitchen. I find her adding bows to six herbal tea jars she's no doubt going to give away. "You know I always find you doing something. Why don't you ever rest or relax for a little?"

She smiles, "I can rest when I'm dead, honey. Besides, there is always something to do." I dismiss myself to use the bathroom and roll my eyes as soon as my back is turned. Stubborn women. My face heats from the memory of when Danny and I were here last.

I hurry to use the bathroom and as I finish, I hear the doorbell ring. No one we know uses the doorbell, so I emerge from the bathroom asking aloud, "Who's that?"

"I don't know," Mamma Cathy responds just as we both walk towards the door.

A second knock comes, and I stand behind Mamma Cathy as she moves to open the door. Standing on the porch is the sheriff, Robert. I remember him from Hazel's baby shower. He's got dark hair and a stocky build. A sad smile plays on his face as he says, "Sorry to disturb you Mrs. Stone but I have some grave news."

I can't see Mamma Cathy's reaction, but she opens the door wider, saying, "It's no problem at all. Nice to see you Robert, please, come in." We move for him to come inside and that's when I notice the small brown box in his hand.

We silently move to the living room and by the time we're all seated my anxiety is heighted, "Is everything okay?" I reach for Mamma Cathy's hand beside me as we sit across from him.

He shakes his head, adjusting the box in his lap, "I'm afraid not. Some out-of-town policemen came to the station today, Cathy, it's about your daughter, Sarah. There's no easy way to say this, but they found her in her apartment, deceased three weeks ago."

My heart drops from his words. Justin's mom? "No, not my Sarah," I hear Mamma Cathy's voice just over a whisper. "I'm so sorry Mrs. Stone." My eyes begin to water, and my stomach turns. I didn't know my aunt too well; she left when we were all kids. Still though, she's family, and now she's gone.

Mamma Cathy's grip in my hand tightens as she replies, "Why didn't anyone call me?"

He replies, "Nobody knew until the landlord called in a welfare check. She died from an overdose and had been dead for at least four days. Since there was no one around, and no contact info, they registered her as a Jane Doe."

I try to silently support my grandmother as her hold on me tightens. She says, "Where is she? We'll go get her."

He finally acknowledges the box in his lap, "After a week went by, she was cremated by the state. Though they were able to find you through her DNA, processing took another week or so. Her and some of her belongings are here." He sets the box on the table between us, "I told them I'd deliver the news personally."

I can see my grandmother fighting back tears as she clears her throat. Robert dismisses himself, "I'll leave you to it, Mrs. Stone. You have my deepest condolences."

He stands and leads himself out of the house. "I am so sorry Mamma Cathy," I say as soon as he leaves. She moves to open the box, speaking barely over a whisper, "Thank you baby."

I watch, holding my breath as she sets the lid down and slowly pulls out a beautiful purple floral vase. Goose bumps cover my skin. *She's in there.* My grandmother sighs, "I tried God, I really did." She's not talking to me, so I remain silent.

When she sets down the vase, I see tears silently falling from her and the sight breaks something in me. My grandmother has always been strong; it takes a lot to make her cry.

Losing a child is sadly something I can relate to, though mine never took its breath. It leaves an emptiness inside you.

I rub one hand on her shoulder, and I hear her cry more, but I don't say anything, allowing her tears to fill the room. Faster than she can collect herself, she's wiping her eyes and telling me she's okay.

She moves to pull out a single picture. I recognize the face of one of the children as my father so the other must be my aunt. Mamma Cathy stands between them. They were kids, no older than ten or eleven, clinging onto Mamma Cathy's side. She was younger too; her grey hair was pitch black, and no wrinkles in sight. They were all happy.

She stares at the picture a moment longer before setting it down and pulling out two envelopes. One had Justin's name on it, and the other had the name Beni. "Who's Beni?" I ask as she sets that one down. "I don't know," She replies, getting ready to open the one with Justin's name on it. "Mamma Cathy! Don't open it, it's not for you."

"Child hush, it came to my house from my daughter, I'm opening it."

Not wanting to push her, I wait as she reveals a letter. I feel like I'm invading so I look away from the letter but still curious I ask, "What's it say?" She doesn't respond Immediately before saying, "I need to go call your father."

As she walks away, I look back at the vase and realize I can't go back to Daniel's yet, not after this, Mamma Cathy needs someone here through all of this. So, I message Daniel, saying we'll talk tomorrow.

He replies almost immediately.

Danny: Lizzy Doll, I don't think I can wait any longer without seeing you.

I smile unwillingly and though I'm still upset with him, I want what we have going on between us. So, I reply:

Me: I'm sure you can. Mamma Cathy shouldn't be alone, my aunt died, it would be horrible of me to leave her right now.

Danny: Fine, if you won't come to me, I'll come to you.

17. Death Comes in Three's

ELIZABETH

It's almost 2 a.m. and I can't sleep.

Part of it has to do with the fact that my aunt's remains are just in the other room. I never got to know her, but seeing Mamma Cathy so upset and hearing my father upset when she called him. It just solidifies that even the strongest women have breaking points.

I toss and turn, eyes closed but restless, a few moments go by before I accept defeat and sit up. Maybe a glass of water will help. I head out of the room and into the kitchen, hating how loud my footsteps sound.

I pull the fridge door open, painstakingly slow, and I grab a glass out of the cabinet at the same pace. When I finally pour the water, I wince at how loud it sounds and wait for a signal that I'm being too loud, but nothing comes. So, I take a few sips of water before taking a deep breath and heading back to the room.

I see my phone screen light up as I climb back in bed, so I grab it and it reads;

My love: You up?

Should I reply and let him know I'm awake or should I ignore him until morning? He knows I can't leave Mamma Cathy alone right now.

The sound of tapping on the bedroom window pulls me from my thoughts. I look towards the window, and I don't see anything, so I don't move. Until I hear the noise again. What the heck is that?

Again, I don't move, I'm not going to end up on the news because I want to play investigator.

My phone pings again.

My love: Lizzy, if you're awake, open the window, it's cold out.

"What the," I whisper to myself as I move out of bed and set my phone down, "No this man is not..." Sure enough when I look out the window, Daniel's looking down at his phone waiting on the other side with a small duffle bag hanging on his shoulder. This man.

I slide the window open, and he looks up from the sound. I notice he took the screen off and when he sees me a grin spreads on his face, "There she is."

"What are you doing here?" I ask, making sure to whisper.

"Well hello to you too," he says as he moves to grip the window seal, and I step back. Is he really about to come in through the window? What kind of high school foolery is happening right now?

He hops up and over, landing louder than I hoped he would. We stay silent a few moments, hoping to God we didn't wake Mamma Cathy.

When I think all is good, I ask again, "What are you doing?"

He answers me while turning to close the window, "I am spending the night with you."

As he turns back to face me, he drops his bag and starts unloading his pockets, setting his phone, wallet, and keys on the end table by the bed. Panic fills as I say, "Are you crazy? Mamma Cathy *does not* play these games. If she finds out you are here, she will literally kill us."

He closes the distance between us not responding to a thing I just said, pulls me into a hug and whispers, "I've missed you so much, Lizzy doll." I should push him away. Tell him I'm still upset with him, and he should leave, but his scent floods my nose and though I mean to pull away, I only pull him closer.

I think I'm still upset with him, but I won't deny that his body feels like home. "I'm still mad at you, you know," I whisper, pulling back to look up at him. He replies, "You can be mad at me all you want Lizzy, but that's not going to change the fact that you're my wife." I give him a pointed look. I'm still shocked by that fact.

"Too soon?" He asks when I don't reply. Taking a deep breath, he pulls me back into him again saying, "Okay, it's too soon, but it's true. You're mine, baby."

I inhale his scent again and a little bit of the reserve I had about us crumbles inside of me. I whisper, "I'm yours."

"Let's get you to bed," He lets go of me, moving to the bed to pull black the blankets for me. I climb in and he slips in behind me, trapping me between him and the wall. I'm still not tired so I stare at the wall and say, "My aunt is dead, and I don't know how to feel about it, I never got to know her."

I feel his body pressed against mine and he wraps his arm around my waist. He kisses the back of my head, whispering, "I'm sorry you didn't get to know her."

I take a deep breath, "It doesn't feel real. We were so young when she left so I only know her by her pictures and some of the stories my dad would tell." He begins rubbing comforting circles on my stomach as I continue, "I don't know how Justin will feel, but I know it hurt Mamma Cathy."

He whispers, "It'll probably hurt your dad too. How'd it happen?"

"She overdosed. What's worse is, nobody knew," I take a deep breath, Danny's presence calming me. "I'm so sorry baby," he says, kissing the back of my head again and pulling me closer.

I feel my body relax, so I finally what's been bothering me the most, "Danny, I want to be yours forever, but I'm scared. So much was happening in our lives when we met, I'm afraid I'm filling a temporary void. I'm afraid that you'll be mine now but what if you wake up and decide you don't want this anymore? That you never did."

I'm afraid of loving him and losing him, wasting more years of my life with someone who doesn't truly want me. He sits up on the bed, and I turn to face him as he says, "Baby you don't know what I've been doing to keep myself from coming over to kidnap you and bringing you back home. Every second of the day since you said you needed space; I've been spinning in circles talking myself into forcing you to stay if you wanted to leave."

He pauses with a laugh before he continues, "Talking myself out of the car with the keys in the ignition. I've been trying to picture my life without you, in case I *had* too, and I couldn't. I'd work myself up all over again and talk myself out of it. It was driving me crazy."

He takes a deep breath, "You have every right to be afraid, but I'll spend every moment of everyday reminding you, you don't have to be. I'm yours, Lizzy until my last breath."

I feel the weight of his words, and I take a deep breath. My sister told me life is all about risk, good or bad. Daniel is worth the risk. "I trust you, Danny. I want this life with you."

I can barely see his face, but I feel the smile in his voice, "and in this life you'll have me. Let's get some sleep, we don't want to wake up late and risk Mamma Cathy finding us." He moves to kiss my head, and I replay his words in my mind, before telling him goodnight.

I wake to see the sun has yet to rise. The weight of Danny's arm still around me fuels me with unexpected happiness. I think he's still asleep, but I feel his cock pressing into my backside. "Danny?" I whisper his name, turning to face him but his eyes are closed and as I listen, he's breathing evenly.

I don't want to wake him, but I certainly don't want Mamma Cathy to get out of bed before we do. I lean down and kiss his lips, before calling his name again. He stirs but doesn't wake, so I move him a little and call him again.

His eyes begin to flutter before blinking a few times. I whisper, "We have to get up." He blinks again, before he moves to rub his eyes. I try to climb over him, to get out of bed but he locks me above him saying, "Not so fast, can't we stay here and cuddle for a while?"

I shake my head and try moving over him again, "No we have to get up before she does." He groans but releases his grip. I climb over him and head to the bathroom; Daniel doesn't follow me in and I'm thankful the house is silent.

When I return to the room, Daniel is sitting on the bed in a fresh shirt and jeans, he pulled from his duffle bag. "I'll go get a pot of coffee started, you go throw your bag in your truck and meet me in the kitchen. He stands saying, "Can I at least brush my teeth?"

"Yeah, just hurry," I say, stepping aside so he can walk past me. As much as I don't want us to get

THE SON OF A GHOST

caught, I am not kissing morning breath Danny all day long. I hurry to the kitchen trying to quiet my steps by walking on my tippy toes. I notice the sun is starting to rise and I begin to panic. I don't actually know when Mamma Cathy wakes up, only that she's always awake before the rest of us.

I fill the kettle with water and place it on the stovetop. A few seconds go by, and Daniel comes walking down the hall, "Going to go toss this in the car." He doesn't wait for my response as he heads for the door. I try to calm down a bit and move to wait at the table. I could cook something for breakfast, but I don't know what mood Mamma Cathy is in and I don't think I can stomach food at the moment.

A couple of minutes later, Danny joins me at the table. He kisses me on the forehead before sitting next to me and I am kind of grateful he's here with me. I can't deny that it's nice having him to lean on. The sun is over the horizon, shining its early morning light as the kettle begins to whistle.

I quickly move to turn off the heat and make Daniel and I a cup of coffee, though I know he's not much of a coffee drinker. Soon I hear Mamma Cathy emerging from her room, her footsteps sound slow and heavy. When she comes into view I greet her with a smile, trying to be positive for her. "Morning Mamma Cathy," I say, and Daniel says the same. "You're awake early," she says, making her way into the kitchen. She notices the kettle on the stove and begins to make herself a cup of coffee.

"We are," I say looking briefly at Daniel before changing the subject, "So, what did Dad say?" She takes a deep breath, adding a teaspoon of sugar into her mug before saying, "He wants her to be buried, but since she's already cremated, I want her here, next to your grandfather's ashes."

That makes sense. I ask, "Are we going to have a funeral for her?" Mamma Cathy shakes her head and finally moves to join us at the table with her cup, "No, she wasn't very popular here in town, I don't want people who didn't care for her to be there. I'd like us to have a private ceremony at the church."

"What about Justin?" I ask, realizing I haven't called him. "He doesn't want to be there," she pauses, deep breathing again before continuing, "I told him he should be, but he said she was never there for him, so why should he be there for her now." His response breaks my heart a little, but I understand.

I feel Danny's hand move to rest on my thigh, and I take comfort in his touch, saying, "So when are we having the ceremony?"

"Hopefully next week, I still have to call Pastor Forkhill to arrange it."

"Okay Mamma Cathy, if there's anything I can do just let me know."

I don't know if it's a coincidence or if death really does come in threes, but after the private funeral we held for my aunt Sarah, a few days later, Daniel's dad died too. The whole town grieves that loss and shortly after that, the town sheriff, Robert, passed away as well.

His death shocked the town. He was healthy as far as anyone knew, but apparently, he had OSA. Sleep Apnea, and because he lived alone, he never knew he had it.

It's been three weeks since we buried his father and in a weird, twisted way all this *death* has made us closer. We're married, though I still haven't told anyone and we're currently in his dad's house cleaning it up. "Danny, I need help!" I yell from the garage trying to pull a heavy box from the top shelf. Daniel comes running in as if screamed for my life saying, "What's wrong?"

With one hand on my hip, I point to the top shelf that's too high for me to reach, saying, "I'd like to pull that box down, but I can't reach it, and you definitely can." He looks at me then at the box, before smiling and stepping in to grab it. With ease he raises his arms and pulls the large cardboard box down.

I thank him with a kiss, "Thanks babe." I notice the box has no writing on it, so I open it. Daniel protests saying, "We're supposed to be packing the house up, not going through everything."

"I can't help it, I'm curious about your childhood home!" I laugh trying to be extra positive because I know this is hard for him.

I continue to open the box and the first thing I see is a black photo album and excitedly I pick it up, "See! Can we look at all of them?" As the words leave my mouth a yellow envelope slips from the album and falls to the floor. Immediately I notice it has Danny's name written on it in black sharpie.

We bend down to pick it up at the same time and he laughs, "You're way more excited about this than you should be." I stand only grinning in response he needs a little sunshine to his rain. He finally grabs the envelope and pulls out a tiny SD card for a camera.

"If that has a bunch of baby photos of you, I totally want to see them."

He smirks, "Too bad, I'm sure this only works with a cam recorder, and we don't have one."

"Fine, challenge accepted." I put the photo album down near the box and begin looking deeper inside of it. If he's got SD cards, he's got to have the camera too somewhere around here.

Just as Danny starts putting the SD card back in the envelope saying, "We'll take it to get uploaded someplace, if you really want to see what's on it."

I yell, "found it!" Excitedly, I pull out a black, old fashioned cam recorder. As I flip the side screen open, Danny can't help but smile as he says, "Okay, you win Lizzy doll. We'll watch whatever is on here, then we'll finish packing up the house."

I nod in agreement, "Deal." He begins to head to the living room, and I grab the photo album before following after him, not wanting it to get lost in another box.

I sit on the couch with the album still in my arms as I watch Danny quickly hook up the old cam. Finally, when it begins to play, he moves to sit next to me. At first, we hear his dad's younger self's voice asking the camera if it's on. Then we see his face.

Daniel's hand rests on my thigh as we take in the youthful Scott McCarter. He has red hair just like Danny and Life to his smile that I've never seen before. We listen as he says, "Today, Daniel started crawling!" As he turns the camera around, we see baby Daniel on the ground and his mother calling out to him, "Come on son, you can do it! Craw to Mamma!"

Her voice takes me by surprise, and I feel Danny's grip on my thigh tighten. She has a wide smile on her face as both she and Scott cheer on baby Danny as he crawls.

Her voice is sweet, soft and encouraging. Unsure of how Daniel's feeling, I quietly set down the photo album and wrap my arms around his.

The clip changes and it starts with Scott's face on the screen. It looks like they're outside in the backyard and he's scrambling to turn the camera around as we hear his moms voice saying, "Hurry honey he's walking! He's actually walking!"

And as the camera turns, we see them sitting on green grass with an orange blanket and a little basket with sandwiches out, Baby Danny's got a piece of bread firm in his grip as he waddles trying to take his first steps to his mom and again her voice surprises me.

By the fifth clip, tears threaten my eyes from the overflow of love I feel pouring out from them as a family. You can feel it through the screen, through the sound of their voices, even though the babble of baby Danny.

When the screen cuts black, I look at Daniel who's wiping tears from his eyes, bent over so his arms rest over his knee. The sight makes my heart burst. I realize this must be hard for him, the wound of losing his dad is still fresh and he must think he's completely alone. Wiping the tears from my own eyes I ask, "Baby, are you okay?" His eyes are red as he replies, "I've never seen these clips before."

I move to sit in front of him on my knees on the floor, squeezing one arm in support, I reply, "You mother seemed like such a happy soul." He gives a broken smile, "Yeah she does."

I move to hug him and no matter what he may think, he's not alone anymore. I'm here, and as long as I am, I don't want him to ever feel alone again. "Have I told you that I love you, Danny?" Still sitting on the couch, with red rimmed eyes, he grins down at me, "No but I'd love to hear you say it again."

I smile moving to spread kisses over his face as I repeat the words, "I. Love. You. Daniel. Mc-

Carter." With my last kiss he hums and pulls me from the floor and into him as he leans back onto the couch. He moves to kiss me on the lips, speaking as if were not alone in the room, his voice barely over a whisper, "I love you too,"

"I'm yours and you're mine." I smile, feeling the love in my chest and all around us.

"Until my last breath, Lizzy Doll."

We kiss again before I move to stand saying, "Let's finish packing up the house."

He sits up but doesn't stand, saying, "You know we don't *have* to sell the house. We could move in and make memories of our own."

A little dumbfounded, I ask, "Are you serious?" Since his father's death he's been adamant on trying to sell it as quickly as possible. "Yeah, I realize though, I don't know her well, this is the house my mother once lived in. My parents raised me here and it's one of the last connections to them, I guess I'm not ready to give that up just yet."

He pauses, standing up and wrapping his arms around my waist as he says, "Plus we can make new memories here too. We can raise our kids in the same bedroom I grew up in, the same backyard and kitchen. This house will be filled with so many memories. Who knows, maybe it'll come alive."

I laugh at that, "Yes to everything but the possibility of a haunted house." He smiles, "What, you don't think it'll make a good attraction someday? I can see it now; tour the haunted house of the McCarter's! Open from Monday to Friday and don't forget to stop at McCarter's Mechanics if you're having a little car trouble!"

We burst out in a fit of laughter, and I say, "You are being so unserious right now!" His grin is so big and after all the gloom, I couldn't be happier than I am right now seeing a smile on his face.

18. Epilogue

ELIZABETH

6 months later

"Six months! We had six months to plan this out and I can't believe I forgot to order a cake! I swear I did though, ugh!" I yell as my heart rate spikes while I try to call Maxxie's Dinner.

"Relax Liz, I can go buy cupcakes, if you want," Hazel says, fixing her curls in the mirror.

"No, I really want a cake," I say, taking a deep breath. I planned out my entire wedding though we agreed on something small, I swore I had every little detail down to a T.

Suddenly I feel like my dress is hugging too tightly and the air is getting hard to breathe. I must be making noise since Hazel's eyes snap over to me before she heads towards me and grabs my arms. "Hey none of that, Liz. Everything will be okay, come on, take deep breaths with me," she says, and I watch mimicking her deep breaths until my heart rate calms down.

There's a knock on the bridal suite door and Clay walks in dressed in a sharp black tux, "Everything okay in here?"

"Yes!" Hazel answers for me as she runs her fingers down the front of her dress. "Well August wanted me to let you know your son needs a diaper change and he changed it last, so I guess it's your turn." Hazel immediately rolls her eyes, but it makes me smile a little. "Carry a man's child for nine months and he still won't take your diaper duty shift. Liz, do not stress yourself out, I'll talk to

THE SON OF A GHOST

Mamma Cathy and see what she can do." She says heading to the door and past Clay.

Clay closes the door and pulls out a bag from behind her and an envelope, "Brian also left this for you. He says thank you for the invite, but he couldn't make it and left you a gift." A little surprised he even responded, I say, "Thank you, can you put it with the others?"

She shakes her head, "He asks if you can open it before you walk down the aisle." Intrigued, I nod, and she hands the envelope over to me and quickly leaves the room.

It reads;

Dear Liz, I want you to know through our marriage I never meant to cause you any harm. We went through a lot together and I still had a lot of learning to do. I want you to know that I am sorry for not being able to be truthful to you or to myself. I am happy to say that I've been attending therapy since our divorce and with each session, I'm growing more comfortable saying that I am a gay man. I hate how our marriage ended, but I'm grateful for the path that it's led me on. I still have love for you and hope one day we can be friends. Congratulations and Cheers to a truly happy marriage.

Tears swell in my eyes as I read the last of his words, I'm happy he's taken the steps to living life as his true self. Maybe I should call him after the wedding.

"Knock, knock," The sound of Danny's voice pulls me from my thoughts, "Lizzy Doll, what's wrong?" As he hurries over to me, I wipe the tears before they can fall saying, "Nothing wrong. What are you doing? You know it's bad luck to see the bride before the wedding."

He doesn't retreat though, pulling me into him, "Baby, we're already married."

"Yeah, yeah I know," I reply as he leans in to kiss me. "But what are you doing here, you're supposed to be waiting at the altar." I realize there's sweat on his forehead, and his body temperature is hotter than normal.

"I came to work out my nerves," he says while moving to kiss my neck. I laugh but make no move to stop him, "We don't have time for you to *work out your nerves*." He pulls back briefly and smiles, "Oh we'll always have time. Bend over the chair."

"We have to be quick," I say with heat blooming within me. I begin to pull up my dress and the thrill of knowing we shouldn't, but we are, has my pussy pulsing. He moves to his knees behind me, and his lips are on mine within seconds, and I gasp before covering my mouth with one hand and supporting my weight with the other.

I feel his tongue spread my lips and I fight back a moan but Danny's not having any of it. He slaps my ass, speaking sternly, "What have I told you before, Lizzy Doll?" I take a deep breath trying to be quiet, "That all my pretty sounds are yours."

"That's right, let me hear them baby," he says before quickly returning to eating my pussy. I don't moan as loud as I want to but loud enough to please him and shortly after, I'm riding out an orgasm while his tongue is deep inside me.

By the third orgasm I'm desperate for his cock to be inside me but he stands, and I turn around to face him, feeling like Jello on my feet. "More. Please More," I beg completely beside myself. He shakes his head before taking a deep breath, "I'd love too, but we have a wedding to attend."

I take a deep breath, feeling more relaxed, "Fine. There will be time to sneak away at some point, right?" He smiles while fixing his tie, "We'll make time." I take another deep breath before he pulls me into him, kissing me hard and passionately. I melt into his arms.

"I love you," he says as he pulls away from me. "I love you more," I reply, watching as he leaves the room. I freshen up one more time, smiling too myself about this new chapter in my life. It's been a rollercoaster, but one I'd gladly ride again if it leads me back to him.

19. Extended Epilogue

DANIEL

Three years later

"Elizabeth McCarter,"

I hear my wife speaking quietly into the phone from the passenger seat. It's been three years since we've been married, and life has been nothing short of adventure. I whisper, "Baby you can make the appointment tomorrow, the girls are fine for now."

The sun is setting and we're currently on the road headed to drop the girls off at the babysitter's house. I look in my rear-view mirror, afraid that simply speaking of them will summon the twins from their slumber. Margo's in the car seat behind me, the reflection from the glass shows that she's still knocked out. Her dark red hair covers her face, her head is tilt and she's holding on to a little teddy bear, and I see her chest rising and falling peacefully.

I glance back at the road before looking at Daniella, who, on the other hand, is laid out wildly in her car seat behind Lizzy. Her legs are up against the backseat, and she's slanted towards the door. Her hair texture is closer to her mom's, so instead of being in her face it's light brown curls are sticking up in the air.

"I know but I'm worried Daniella will need glasses baby. She's squinting too much, even when objects are near her face," Lizzy expresses as she hangs up the phone and regrips the pan of peach cobbler in her lap with one hand while a smaller tub rest on top of it. Then she uses the other to rub her growing belly. My heart feels full as I reach to rub my hand on her belly too, "and if she needs glasses, then we'll get her glasses but for now, she's okay Lizzy."

I glance at the road again, noticing that we're almost at the babysitter's house. She agrees looking back at the girls herself before saying, "How'd we get so lucky." Her smile is contagious, and I reply, "I don't know, I blame your grandmother's tea."

She laughs at this and soon we're pulling into the babysitter's driveway. Lizzy watches as I wake the twins and get them unbuckled and out of the car. Margo chooses to walk but Daniella insists I carry her, and Lizzy only laughs.

She's been clingy since we told them they were getting a baby brother. Lizzy takes Margo's hand while I carry Daniella and their bags as we walk to the porch. I don't have to ring the doorbell as the front door swings open revealing Annie's wide smile. "You made it!" She greets and Margo runs into her arms. I try to put Daniella down saying, "Look where we are, freckles. Annie is excited to see you."

It takes five minutes to convince her to get down but once she's on the ground her and her sister run to the backyard where I know the swing set is. "Thanks again for watching them," Lizzy says as she hugs her goodbye.

"Nonsense, I'm always available to watch the girls," Annie replies. "Here's a piece of the Mama Cathy's peach cobbler you wanted," Lizzy says handing her the small container of pie. Annie's face lights up, "I cannot wait to devour this!"

"You and Caleb!" Lizzy laughs. Annie sets the plate down inside and waves us towards the car, "Now go have fun!". We thank her again before walking back to the car. I move to open the car door for Lizzy as she resets the main container of cobbler in her lap again. Then I head to the driver's side.

Tonight's one of our *adults only* get togethers. This time it's being hosted by August and Hazel. As I climb into the car, my phone dings with a text from August in our group chat reading:

August: you fuckers on your way?

Me: We're on the way now, don't drink all the beer without me!

Caleb: Don't get your boxers in a twist, heading out the door now.

I pocket my phone and start the car, saying, "That was August, he's rushing us as usual." Lizzy laughs while putting on her seatbelt and we take off.

"Hi!"

"Hey!" Hazel and Lizzy greet each other on the porch. As soon as Hazel sees the cobbler though she releases Lizzy saying, "Ooh let me get the first bite! God knows when Caleb gets here, he'll try to take the whole thing home!" She takes the dish as Lizzy agrees, and they head into the kitchen. I see a lit fire in the backyard and head that way instead.

"About time!" August shouts standing from his chair around the fire to greet me. "The man of the hour has arrived!" I reply with sarcasm, pulling him into a brief hug before doing the same with Larson, his brother. We aren't that close but he's a friend no less.

"So, where's the beer?" I ask, taking a seat next August. Larson pulls a twelve pack from the floor beside him, saying, "I've got it." He begins to open the pack and hand each of us one. It's not as cold as I'd like, but I reply, "Thanks. Though it probably won't last the night."

August replies, "Well that depends if Caleb wants a rematch on that drinking game or not."

"You know he will," Larson says, taking a sip of his beer. I hear Lizzy and Hazel slide open the back door to come join us outside. I stand to help Lizzy sit in the chair beside me and she asks for the chips and dip near the table.

Resting one hand on her belly we continue our conversation, and I take a deep breath feeling the warmth in my chest. I can't believe I thought I'd be alone in this world. The shop is doing well; my best friends are still assholes. I've got a beautiful wife, two kids and another on the way. I look to the stars, taking a sip of my beer while thinking to myself; you were right dad, you were so fucking right.

Author's Note

Sweet baby Jesus I never thought this book would see the light. This book was cut shorter than I intended. As much as I loved Daniel and Elizabeth's story it got harder to continue towards the end for multiple reasons, but mainly because this trilogy is very lightweight aka, we're here for a good time not a long time.

The first thing I want to talk about from their story is about Lizzy's ex-husband, Brian. I didn't want to make him a villain, but I did have to make him just a little salty. On a serious note, though, I've been around firsthand to see people I love struggle with their sexuality, there's pressure from the outside to remain something you're not and the pressure from the inside of having to hide who you are. I can acknowledge that the world can be cruel, so it's completely okay not to talk about it if you're not ready, just know I'm here for you when you are.

I want to make it abundantly clear that Brian wasn't the villain because he is gay, but because he hurt those closest to him and himself. Entering a marriage, you know you're not truly committed too, knowing you barely wanted to touch them, making them believe something is wrong with them, was not only hurtful to Elizebeth but to himself. It was really important to me that their friendship could be rectified even after all the drama as he wasn't a bad person, just someone who made a bad choice.

Next, I'd like to talk about how I swear Daniel McCarter sometimes had a mind of his own. As hard as I tried to give him the dark romance vibe like August and Caleb, I simply could not. Though he was definitely putting the P in pleasure for our girl Lizzy.

I want to take a moment to thank my *whole* street team. I struggled really hard during the months it took to write this book and every time I popped back in; you guys supported me like I never left. So, I am forever grateful for you guys!

Now that I've finally finished The Son of a Ghost, I realized I have a few things to say about book 1 The Son of a Pastor (TSOAP). When I wrote that story it was originally supposed to be a standalone novel, but I fell in love with August, Daniel, and Caleb and wanted to see them all get happy endings.

When I wrote TSOAP it felt like a fever dream honestly, I completed the first draft in four months. Wild, I know, but now here we are at the end of book two. Though I tried to pipe down the spice, it's still heavily spicy, and I'm okay with that. If open door and plentiful isn't for you, that's okay too.

The book covers, oh my goodness! I took so long creating the covers for Book 2 *and* Book 3. I started with a blank white page, made pretty covers then changed it, *liked it,* then changed it again! I love discrete covers, so I am so happy with the final outcome! The Son of a Pastor's cover was not made by me (It was a cover template and no, it was not

AI generated), so The Son of a Ghost and book three's covers definitely hold a special place in my heart.

At the end of the day, I want the Springville Trilogy to be a fun and spicy read so if you enjoyed it this far, Thank you! I appreciate your support more than you'll ever know and if you didn't, thank you anyway for giving my book a try!

About the Author

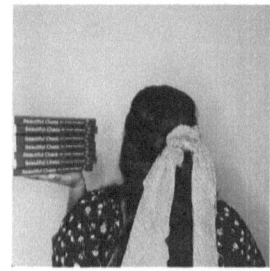

Amber Rodriguez is a spicy romance author who lives in California. She likes reading in her free time, slow mornings, and all things nature and cottage core inspired. She's a sucker for spicy romance books and a mild coffee addict!

If you'd like to connect with her, you can find her on;

Website: www.amrbooks.com

On Instagram @booksbyamber118

On TikTok @booksbyamber118

On Facebook @Author Amber Rodriguez

The Son of a Ghost Discussion Guide

Now that you've made it to the end of the story, Share your thoughts!

1. Is the first scene captivating?

2. Was the conflict/tension enough to maintain your interest?

3. Who was your favorite character and why?

4. Was there any characters you liked/dislike, and why?

5. Did the ending bring the story to a satisfactory conclusion?

6. Did you think about the story when you were away from it? What did you think about?

7. What parts are the most memorable?

8. Final thoughts

www.ingramcontent.com/pod-product-compliance
Lightning Source LLC
LaVergne TN
LVHW091713070526
838199LV00050B/2383